M.K. MACLEAN

Kryda's Beginnings

Book 1 of Kryda's Adventures

Copyright © 2021 by M.K. MacLean

All rights reserved. No part of this publication may be reproduced, stored or transmitted in any form or by any means, electronic, mechanical, photocopying, recording, scanning, or otherwise without written permission from the publisher. It is illegal to copy this book, post it to a website, or distribute it by any other means without permission.

This novel is entirely a work of fiction. The names, characters and incidents portrayed in it are the work of the author's imagination. Any resemblance to actual persons, living or dead, events or localities is entirely coincidental.

M.K. MacLean asserts the moral right to be identified as the author of this work.

First edition

Editing by Danielle Corbet
Cover art by CalicoSushi

This book was professionally typeset on Reedsy.
Find out more at reedsy.com

Contents

Acknowledgement		v
Dedication		vi
1	Chapter 1	1
	The Homestead	1
2	Chapter 2	13
	The Journey	13
3	Chapter 3	23
	The Beast Slayer	23
4	Chapter 4	36
	The Villagers	36
5	Chapter 5	55
	The Lower City	55
6	Chapter 6	64
	The Adventurers	64
7	Chapter 7	72
	The Bargain	72
8	Chapter 8	81
	The Inn	81
9	Chapter 9	90
	The Orientation	90
10	Chapter 10	102
	The Mission	102
11	Chapter 11	113
	The Urgrosh	113
12	Chapter 12	119
	The Old Man	119
13	Chapter 13	126
	The Sewers	126

14	Chapter 14	142
	The Retreat	142
15	Chapter 15	152
	The Return	152
16	Chapter 16	161
	The Final Battle	161
17	Chapter 17	173
	The Disappearance	173
About the Author		180

Acknowledgement

There are many people to thank for this book coming to pass. My first Nano-Wrimo partner Lennox Lepage, my dreaming partner Amy Jefferson, my husband and DM Jamie MacLean for helping these characters come to life over and over again. To many other DMs and playing partners who created the banter and laughs throughout the campaigns. Foremost, to my editor, Danielle Corbette for the enthusiasm and dedication in making this book a reality.

Dedication

To my father, Ronald Gostick, who passed away before he could see this journey and who always encouraged me to do what I love.

Chapter 1

The Homestead

Kryda stood facing the watery entrance to the cave, her unruly auburn hair damp on her shoulders. Despite the chill, a small fire warmed the cave, and after a long morning of working a heavy pickaxe—and then the usual noontime fun with her working partner, best friend and lover, Fáelán—Kryda's back was moist with sweat. As she idly tugged her shirt back over her head, she turned to face Fáelán.

He was lying on his side next to their small fire, head propped up on one arm, staring adoringly at Kryda. He pouted playfully when she covered herself, but then smiled up at her fondly. He was tall and gangly by dwarven standards, but what he lacked in bulk, he made up for in definition. The muscles in his supporting arm rippled invitingly as he shifted towards her, gently stroking her arm with his calloused fingertips. Kryda sighed. This was not going to be easy. Her thick dwarven accent echoed softly as she broke the silence.

"Look, Lan, this is fun and all, but please understand that it cannae be more. Ye know I dunae want that kind of life."

Fáelán rolled his eyes at her and sat up. "We've been through this a million times. O' course it'll be more. The elders are nae so stupid as tha', they already know about us. After the ceremony tomorrow, ye won't have much of a choice anyhow, will ya?" Fáelán teased. He stood and pulled his own shirt back on, an excited gleam in his eye. "They'll have us betrothed on the spot and our hands'll be tied wit'in the year."

A small smile tugged at the corners of her lips at his enthusiasm, but Kryda remained silent. Fáelán merely sighed and turned away, snatching his trousers off the rocky ground and irritably tugging them back over his stout legs. "Wish ye didn't have to be *told* to take me as yer fáerkéile," he muttered.

Kryda didn't quite catch what he said, but she knew him well enough to have a pretty good idea. A little sadness touched her eyes, but she recovered before he could see. As she pulled her boots back on and reached for her pick, she shrugged. "It won't matter by then."

"What do you mean by that?!" Lan whirled back to face her, looking as if she might as well had struck him. Kryda returned his shocked stare and squared her jaw.

"I'm leaving."

"What?! Leaving where? The cave? Ye cannae possibly mean yer leavin' the village! Where would ye be goin? Yer not even an adult yet!"

At his reaction, Kryda's resolve wavered. She softened her voice, but she wasn't going to back down. "I'm as good as."

"Then ye could start actin' it!" he spat, rolling his eyes and then bending down to retrieve his own pickaxe.

Kryda gritted her teeth at the blow, but continued as if he hadn't said anything. "Ye said yourself, I'll be acknowledged tomorrow, but then what? More o' this?" She gestured vaguely at the cave they'd found as kids. It was richer in resources than all of the mines near the village combined, and had made their families quite wealthy. They'd never told anyone where it was, but ever since they'd found it, they both knew they would take up the pick and work in this cave together one day.

CHAPTER 1

"Would that really be so bad?" Lan pouted. As he looked back up at her, Kryda could see the pain in his glazed eyes. "We've got more here than anyone in our village has had in generations! And we have each other."

Kryda sighed and turned away. "I know there's a lot here for me, Lan. I'm not saying there isn't. But there's somethin' out *there*, too. I can feel it...a grand adventure!"

There was the excitement Lan had feared he would see. He had always known that Kryda would be hard to settle down with, but he thought by now she'd have gotten over her childish ideas.

"I dunnae know what it is yet," Kryda continued, her eyes focused on something distant that Fáelán couldn't see. "But I know it's waiting for me. I have to at least try to find it, Lan. I've got to go. I don't belong here...at least, not yet."

Lan broke at last. He lurched forward and wrapped his arms around her tightly, holding her, trying to keep her there, with *him*. "You belong with me!" he cried, tears spilling from his eyes.

Kryda turned to face him, fighting back the mist that formed in her own eyes at the sight of his tears. She looked deep into his forest-green eyes, her emerald gaze searching his own, and reached up to touch his face, brushing the tears away gently. She couldn't speak around the lump in her throat; all she could do was slowly shake her head.

Lan's eyes searched hers for a few more moments. Then, breathing heavily, his nostrils flaring, he pulled roughly away from Kryda and flung his pickaxe to the earth. Biting back his tears, he leaped into the underground lake, plunging deep into the water and swimming furiously towards the mouth of the cave. Kryda flinched at the splash; she was sure that if there had been a door, he'd have slammed it.

Choking back a sob, she sat back down by the little fire, and noticed he'd left his pickaxe. His name was carved into the handle, the first modification any dwarf made to their pickaxe when they were presented with it on the first day of Trials. She traced the letters with her fingers, then clutched the tool to her chest and finally allowed herself to cry.

KRYDA'S BEGINNINGS

* * *

They had played together as children, following their parents on some of the shorter mining trips and pretending to find rare, or rather imaginary, gems as they tapped on the stone walls with sticks. Kryda was always the more adventurous of the pair, wandering off to find new and exciting places to hide and play. She would often come home with strange and beautiful geodes, carelessly flaunting the fact that she had gone well beyond where she should have been.

Kryda was an insatiable explorer, and after eventually accepting that she completely refused to be confined to the boundaries of the village, her father decided to train her extensively in survival skills. The one thing he couldn't teach her, though—the secret that no one in her village knew—was how to swim. The dwarves of her village would only wade just deep enough to fill a bucket of water when it was needed, and that was only if there hadn't been enough rain to keep their storage tanks filled. Kryda had been the first to overcome the deep-seated distaste and fear of open water, but she had learned the hard way.

Kryda and Lan had ventured forth on yet another adventure, Kryda bold as ever and Lan trying to convince her to head back. She had been inching closer to a coveted spot for months, following the flow of a stream that often brought glimmering flecks into the village. The other miners didn't think it was worth looking into for such tiny flecks, and the scouts had never found anything worthwhile in that direction, but Kryda knew that the years of tiny flecks sparkling in the stream had to have come from something bigger. Her travels had led her to a huge rocky outcropping, overlooking a lake so wide that the far shores were barely visible from the cliff on which she stood—the same lake that fed the small cove near her village.

On the day Kryda finally made it to the mouth of the little stream at the base of the outcropping, she was not disappointed. There were indeed some rich resources in those rocks. Delighted, she decided to mine a sample to take back to the village. She had come prepared for such a task, of course—her

CHAPTER 1

father had given her his old pickaxe, even though she wasn't yet officially old enough to choose her trade. Of course, her father hadn't had much choice in the matter, since Kryda would take it from the rack every chance she got. When he had finally given in and let her take it as her own, she had immediately marked her name under his with her mother's sticks of colored beeswax.

On the top of the ledge, but feeling as if she were on top of the world, Kryda aimed her pickaxe at a chunk of ore so big she would have a hard time carrying it back without a cart. At least, it seemed a substantial piece, in comparison to her own childlike frame. Lan, cautious as ever, had begged her to come down before the rocks gave way into the water, but Kryda was determined to chip out that ore.

When the pickaxe struck, the sound rang deep and metallic over the lake. Kryda stopped to listen to it ripple across the water and back again. As the initial echoes died down, she noticed there was a lower rumbling as well, coming from below. She put her ear to the rock and waved away another protest from Fáelán, whose pleading was growing more urgent. The rumbling didn't last long, but she thought she could hear water splashing and dripping. With her ear still to the stone, she lifted her pick and struck again, this time slightly to the side of the chunk of ore. Her pickaxe sank deep into the rock, and the rumbling began again, followed by the 'plunk' of stones falling into water, but the sounds were all muffled echoes. Kryda's eyes suddenly widened as she realized what that meant.

"Fáelán! Did ye hear tha'?! The echoing—do ye know what that means?! It's a cave, Fáelán! A new cave! I'll bet it has more ore than we can fit in our pouches!" Kryda exclaimed in youthful exuberance. She sprinted back up to the edge. "We have got to be findin' the way in!"

"Kryda! Slow down, please!" Fáelán called after her, climbing carefully up behind her. "There probably isn't a way in. Scouts have come through here before and found nothin' but rock. I'm tellin' you—"

Kryda flopped down on her stomach and peered over the edge of the cliff, tapping her pickaxe and listening for weak spots, anything that would tell her how to get in. Just then, the moss gave way under Kryda, and she slipped over the edge. She grasped at the shrubs growing from the side, scrambling for something to hold on to, but they were not strongly rooted in the rough stone, and each one broke away as easily as the moss had. Just before Kryda hit the water, she glimpsed Lan leaning over the side of the cliff, his eyes wide with terror, one arm stretched out as if to catch her.

The icy cold of the water tugged at her, stealing the breath from her chest. She struggled to swim, but this was the first time she'd been in water deeper than her knees, and she'd never seen anyone else swim. Besides, she was still carrying a heavy pickaxe. As her muscles began to give out from lack of oxygen, she released her pickaxe, idly watching it fall as her mind and vision darkened. Somewhere in the back of her mind she saw it settle onto the bottom of the lake, right next to a dark hole in the cliff face. Kryda knew she should be excited for some reason, but her world was growing steadily darker, and she couldn't think of anything but the sudden rush of cold in her chest and the shadow descending over her.

* * *

Kryda shook off the memory as she slowly gathered the rest of the things Fáelán had left behind as he'd stormed out of the cave. With a pickaxe on either hip and a waterproof bag treated with animal fat slung over her shoulder, she slipped into the water and swam out of the mouth of the cave. She pulled herself out of the lake, idly wrung the worst of the dampness from her shirt, and strolled home slowly, enjoying what would likely be her last walk through this trail.

She didn't even notice the encroaching twilight until she heard two clear blasts of a horn. It was her mother's signal, one she'd begun using when Kryda had started to wander further than a shout would carry. Kryda fumbled through her bag for her own instrument and hastily sounded two blasts in return to let her mother know that she was well and on her way home. Breaking into a sprint, she ran the rest of the way back to the village, knowing

CHAPTER 1

that every moment spared by her haste was one less moment of the inevitable maternal lecture she'd have to endure upon her return.

The moment Kryda stepped through the door, her mother rushed to scold her. "Kryda! Where have ye been, dear? When we saw Fáelán come back in such a sour mood, we thought you'd not be far behind ranting about his cautious nature as usual." Turning briefly to her husband, she murmured to him, "You'd think after tha' time when they were wee that she'd ha' learnt to be more prepared herself." Whirling back upon an impatient Kryda, she complained, "You know, we was worried sick all that night ye stumbled intae the lake. We sounded the horn, ye did nae answer. We sent scouts fer ya, but even the dogs lost the trail at the rocks and it was too dark for them poor people to see the-"

"Yes, mum," Kryda broke in, "I know. You were so scared ya hardly let me leave the house for a week and even then, you'd come running after me down the path. If it wasn't for da-"

"I think that'll be enough reminiscin' fer tonight," her father interrupted, quickly changing the subject. "Come, dear, ye need yer sleep." He put his arm around his wife and smiled at her affectionately, the corners of his eyes crinkling.

"You're right m'dear, it's late. All is well now, tha's what matters. G'night, me wee gem." Mother gave Kryda a hug and a kiss on the cheek before heading to her bedroom.

Father followed, but not before shooting Kryda a pointed look to remind her of their promise NOT to tell mother that he'd purposely distracted her so Kryda could 'escape'. Kryda smiled cheekily back at him. "G'night, mum 'n da. Sleep well."

As Kryda sat quietly, waiting for the kettle to boil for her evening tea, she noticed that there was still a candle burning in Lan's room across the way. She suddenly wanted nothing more than to go to him, to fall into his arms and seek his comfort, but knew that would only make this harder. Absorbed in his flickering shadow as it paced back and forth, Kryda didn't notice the water in the kettle boiling over until the figure suddenly stopped. Lan must have felt that he was being watched. Kryda ducked out of sight, then quickly blew out her candle and finished preparing her tea by the light of the moon. She carried the tea to her room and sipped it thoughtfully until she was sure that everyone, including Lan, was fast asleep.

After packing a single change of clothes and three days worth of food, Kryda strapped her pickaxe to her hip and covered herself in her sturdiest cloak, carefully adjusting the hood to shroud her face. On her way out, she contemplated taking Lan's pickaxe back to him. She crept across the way to his door, but as she was about to leave the pickaxe on his doorstep, she stopped. Instead, she pulled her own out of the belt loop and propped it up beside the door, then strapped his to her hip. After glancing up at his window one last time, she slipped into the shadows.

* * *

Fáelán couldn't sleep. He was sure Kryda had been watching him, but when he glanced over at her window, there were no candles burning and all seemed quiet. *Maybe she changed her mind and decided to stay after all*, he thought. He kept watch by the window for as long as he could keep his eyes open, but the afternoon had taken more out of him than he'd realised, and he drifted off on the window ledge with his head on his arms.

His sleep slowly filled with dreams, the worst he'd had since he was a mere lad. Kryda, lost in the bush and starving. Kryda fending off a vicious animal, her strong arms torn and bloodied. Kryda ripping his chest open, tearing his heart out with a fist as she laughed at his foolish affections. Kryda in the arms of some foreign man. Kryda, heavy with child, whispering, "I'll never leave you, my fáerkéile," then fading away. Of all the horrors he'd experienced, that one was the worst. It seemed so real, warmth and hope filling his chest as he gazed at his beloved, but it was all ripped away when he woke with a start, sweating profusely.

As his pounding heart slowly regained its normal rhythm, Fáelán's grip on reality returned, and he soon realized that his brief lull into sleep might have

CHAPTER 1

caused him to miss Kryda's departure. He stared out the window, scrutinizing the familiar house and holding in a panicked breath, but he didn't see or hear anything. Hoping that the stillness meant all was well after all, he sighed in relief.

But as he stood up to blow out the candle, something down below caught the light of the moon. He couldn't make out what it was, but he knew there hadn't been anything there earlier. He'd missed something. With tears already threatening to overwhelm him again, he stumbled down to the front door and threw it open. His eyes caught the pickaxe on his doorstep. Snatching it up, he ran his fingers over the engraving of Kryda's name, and agony gripped him. He glanced around frantically, but there was no one in sight. Collapsing to his knees, Fáelán threw back his head in rage and screamed her name.

* * *

Kryda stumbled through the woods, twigs snapping underfoot, her cloak catching on bushes. Panting heavily, her mind raced through her plan of escape. If she could just make it to her first hideout, she'd be in the clear. No one, not even Lan, had known of this spot. She'd used it when they were kids to win at hide and seek, which had been a little unfair since most of the other children were too afraid to stray that far from the village. She hadn't purposely kept it from Lan—she hadn't even thought about it in years—but now, she was glad it was still her secret.

Almost there, Kryda thought to herself. *Just a little longer, and then freedom.* She paused briefly to catch her breath, leaning forward, her hands on her knees. A light breeze rustled the leaves around her, the silence broken only by the chirps and calls of woodland creatures.

Then the scream of something terribly wounded ripped through the silence, and Kryda felt as if her heart would stop. It was Lan, bellowing her name, and the despair in his cry was like a knife in her chest. She had never, in all her time spent with the best friend she had in all the world, heard his voice so broken with utter betrayal. Gasping for air, sobs racking her body, Kryda's resolve wavered. She crumpled to her knees and wept like a babe.

It was the sound of her mother's horn, followed by the distant shouts of searching villagers, that finally tugged her back to her feet and spurred her forward again. Kryda was exhausted, physically and emotionally, but she knew her pursuers were getting closer by the moment. She peered back at the path she'd taken, inspecting the trail she'd left them to follow. Satisfied, she stepped out of the forest and onto the hard-packed road that wound through the woods, towards the gates of the dwarven territory. The searchers would expect her to be heading this way, but with any luck, her tracks would vanish in the travel-worn road.

However, Kryda noticed that some bits of her cloak had been torn off by the bushes, and she knew that she couldn't be careless enough to leave any more traces. Despite the chill of the night, she shed her cloak and crammed it hastily into her pack—there was that problem solved. She followed the road for a short while, then plunged back into the bushes, this time being more careful about leaving a trail.

When she finally emerged from the forest again, she was greeted by the welcome sight of the sturdy outer wall that surrounded the dwarven lands, snaking across a bumpy ridge of hills that lent extra height to the barrier. Dotted along the hills, just inside the wall, were crumbling clusters of abandoned dwarven hovels. This was where her village had begun centuries ago, before constant wars forced her ancestors to abandon the top of the ridge and instead retreat behind it for safety. They had constructed the long wall atop the ridge, then dug a tunnel through the largest hill to allow the road through it, instead of over it, and barred the tunnel with sturdy wooden gates.

As a result of these fortifications, not much was left of the old hovels. Most had collapsed entirely into piles of rubble, with only a few chimney stones left standing to speak of olden days. Kryda's keen eyes scanned the ruins until she spotted her hideout—a particularly miniature hovel, surprisingly sturdy in comparison to the rest, squatting atop a nondescript hill to the east

CHAPTER 1

of the tunneled gates.

While exploring the ridge as a child, Kryda had quickly discovered why this particular small hut had not shared the same fate as the rest. The village elders had told stories of a crazy old inventor that once lived among her people, an elderly gnome who had kept mostly to himself. Once in a while, though, the villagers would hear small explosions from his home, or the little tinkerer would run about the village showing off his newest inventions.

The dwarves rarely had any use for his fancy gadgets, but visiting traders of other races seemed to like them, and the old gnome never did anyone any harm—in fact, he was particularly beloved by the dwarven children, whom he would sometimes indulge with gifts of intricate little toys. No one knew why he had chosen to live with the dwarves in the first place, instead of among his own people, but he seemed content. However, luckily for Kryda, he had not been content to adopt their architectural habits, and had chosen to construct his home of mostly metal instead of wood and stone, and added many little oddities to keep the little hut snug and strong. This is what gave Kryda her hiding place.

Kryda clambered up the hill, seeking the secret entrance she knew was there. Nestled between a couple of large slabs of rock were the remnants of the gnome's strange sky window. The glass had shattered long ago as the ground shifted from the collapsing structures nearby, but the metal frame surrounding it remained in place and provided an opening to the hovel.

Kryda slipped tentatively into the opening, taking special care not to cut herself on the remaining rose-colored fragments of glass, and curled up in a dark, sheltered corner of the hut. Even though she was still sweating profusely from the run through the bush, she felt a chill run down her spine. She was scared. Scared of leaving, scared of being found and forced to return, scared to face Fáelán. Shivering, she pulled out her cloak and wrapped it snugly around herself, trying to forget the deep pain tugging at her heart. Despite Kryda's many layered exhaustion, sleep eluded her for several long hours. It wasn't until the muffled sounds of a search passed by and faded that sleep finally, mercifully, overtook her.

KRYDA'S BEGINNINGS

2

Chapter 2

The Journey

Kryda's sleep was plagued with nightmares, playing out every possible scenario that could unfold from this turning point in her life. In one, she turned back, stayed in her village and married Lan. It seemed sweet enough, but the deep sense of failure and unfulfilled destiny was just as terrible as the fear that filled her now. In the next dream, she awoke with no fear of her upcoming journey and continued confidently through the forest—until she was brutally attacked by a wolf. The beast leapt at her and knocked her to the earth, tearing at her face and arms, but then sat back and merely watched with dark eyes as she slowly bled to death.

The dream changed again, and Kryda saw her mother stricken with grief. Fearful of her daughter's fate, she fell deathly ill, but no one could find Kryda to tell her, to beg her to come home. As her mother faded away, her father descended into madness, and Lan, accepting Kryda's demise, married someone he hated. He took to drinking and began beating his new partner, the drinking and beatings growing in severity together over time. The whole village seemed to have fallen into some horrible state of wrath, and the young ones wandered off, only to be consumed by the forest, never to return. They all blamed Kryda for starting the madness, and when she returned at last, they demanded her head on a spike instead of giving her the hero's welcome she'd been expecting.

When Kryda finally awoke, she was sweating so profusely that her cloak had soaked through, and was rapidly giving her a chill. She wanted so badly to kindle a fire, but if she intended on continuing her escape, she had to be further away before she could risk it. She flipped her cloak inside out so the drier side was against her, and gathered her things, hastily chewing a piece of jerky. She carefully made her way out of the hole that used to be the strangest home in a forgotten village, and now sheltered an adventurer whose life would, perhaps, be stranger still.

The sun was barely peeking over the horizon, but Kryda could hear the search party regrouping in the distance, intent upon finding her before she escaped their reach. If she'd slept any longer, she'd have had to stay hidden for most of the day, if not all. She quickly realized that she'd have to move much more quickly if she were to escape, and scrambled hurriedly up the hill, over the wall, and down the far edge of the barricade that sheltered her little village from the rest of the world.

As soon as her feet touched the road, she ran, no longer paying any heed to her tracks. The search party would resume where they'd lost her trail last night, but it would take them a while to make their way past the gates, and longer still to rediscover her tracks that far down the road. By then, wind, wildlife, and perhaps a cart or two would have obscured them to the point where no one would suspect she had come that way. *If I catch one of the carts on their way through, I might even be able to hitch a ride*, she mused. Breathing heavily, she slowed back to a walk, content that she was almost entirely free of her pursuers, and turned back into the woods to find a place to make camp.

CHAPTER 2

* * *

After finding a suitable clearing to set up camp, Kryda hunted some small game for dinner, and then finally sat down for a much-needed meal and some rest. She gazed idly up at the sky in the direction she was headed and finally allowed herself to dream of the freedom she was chasing. She smiled to herself around a mouthful of game, idly toying with Lan's pickaxe as she ate. "Happy Acknowledgement, Lan," she said aloud. "No matter where me travels take me, the axe will always be a part of me. As will you be. There was ne'er any question o' that."

After finishing her meal, she stared into the low flames, sipping a flagon of mead and thinking about her next move. She'd be coming up to the crossroads tomorrow, and she'd have to decide: North to the small human village, or East to the gnomish capital. Her wineskin was almost empty, and it was a long way to the gnomish capital, but at least she'd be assured some decent drink when she did get there. Gnomish capital it was, then.

She'd just begun packing her things when she heard a commotion from the road. Hastily stamping out what was left of her fire, Kryda stashed her belongings in a hollow tree nearby and quietly went to investigate, hoping these were travelers heading toward the gnomish city. As she approached, keeping carefully behind the thick foliage at the edge of the road, she recognized the voices as dwarven and stayed her approach. She could hear them well, but could not see from the bushes, so she climbed a stout tree to observe from above.

"We should be gettin' back. It's almost dark and there's been no sign of her. I'm tellin' ye, she's hopped a wagon. She's long gone by now," sighed one dwarf.

The other stood quietly for a moment and looked around, carefully surveying the area before replying. "It's been windy enough to blow away shallow tracks, but not enough to cover that of a wagon wheel." He knelt, briefly inspecting the earth, then shook his head. "There's been no wagons on this road fer about a week, which means there will be one soon; tomorrow at the latest, most like. If we don't find her tonight, then she really will be gone."

Kryda recognised these dwarves. She knew the first one was the son of the tailor, but she couldn't recall his name. His father had died of some illness when he was young, and ever since, he'd always been very quiet and nervous. He'd follow like a shadow behind the second dwarf, a young rip called Grick. Grick's mother was the best blacksmith the village had, and his father was the second. Young Grick was just the opposite of the tailor's son; a headstrong daredevil who was never afraid of a scrap. The other dwarf children had always teased him that he must be half orc, but he seemed to take that as a compliment. Grick and his shadow were always inseparable, and Grick treated him like a little brother, always trying to toughen him up. It never worked.

Kryda knew her former playmates posed no threat. She slid quietly down the tree and started back to her camp, deciding to head deeper into the forest just to be safe. But just before she was out of earshot, she heard a third voice—one she could never mistake. Her eyes widening, Kryda crept back to the cover of the brush.

"Stop yer bickerin' already. We *will* find her. Tonight." The third dwarf hadn't raised his voice at all, but the tone was menacing enough that Grick and his companion flinched like he'd cracked a whip. They nodded meekly, and continued their search for the trail.

Kryda was frozen to the spot. What had she done? That voice…it was so harsh, one she never would have associated with her best friend. Her eyes widened as his name involuntarily escaped her lips.

"Lan!"

Realizing what she'd done, she clapped a hand over her mouth, and crumpled to the ground.

* * *

CHAPTER 2

Kryda lay curled up in the brush, her sides heaving, lost in a haze of half-formed thoughts. A wet spot on her face brought her back to reality, and she reached up to brush it from her cheek. *Was I cryin'?* she thought. *Why would I be...?* Another drop smacked her forehead, and she realized that it was beginning to rain. She hadn't even noticed it coming in.

Lan... she sighed. *How long have I been lyin' here?* The clouds shrouding the sun made it nearly impossible to tell, but it wasn't dark enough to be night just yet. She glanced cautiously out towards the road, peeking through the bushes. The dwarves had gone. She slowly picked herself up off the ground, stretched, and took a deep breath to steady herself. With one last look toward the last place she'd ever hear Lan's voice, she headed back to her camp.

Her fire pit was still warm enough that rekindling the flames was no difficult task, but the rain was coming down harder by the moment, so she gathered some materials for a simple lean-to just big enough for her and the fire. Hunger gnawed at her stomach, so some hours must have passed since she'd seen Lan and his patrol on the road, but she didn't have the energy to go hunting again—especially not in this weather.

Kryda retrieved some dried berries and meat from her pack, along with a crust of bread. She ate mechanically, without tasting any of it. When she finished, she lay down to try and catch some sleep. As she closed her eyes, a drop trickled down the side of her face. This time it wasn't the rain.

* * *

Kryda awoke to a warm, sloppy wetness licking the drops from her cheeks. She wiped her face irritably and opened her eyes to see a large silver-grey dog sitting in front of her, its big blue eyes peering curiously into her own. She wondered sleepily who it belonged to; she'd never seen this particular dog around the village before.

As she became more aware of her surroundings, she realized she wasn't in the village at all and must have fallen asleep out in the forest. *What's a dog doin' way out here?* she wondered. Then she remembered—she was nowhere near the village. She sat up with a start and stared intently at the dog that was now looming over her, impossibly huge. Kryda gasped at the sudden and terrifying realization that she was under the very careful scrutiny of a wolf. She tried to scramble away, but her back thumped heavily against a tree. The wolf stepped forward to follow, and Kryda froze.

Heart pounding, she held up a hand toward the massive animal and murmured soothingly, desperately hoping the wolf would stay calm. Or maybe she was trying to talk herself into being calm, since the wolf was displaying nothing more than a mild curiosity, at least for the moment. They stared at each other for what felt like half a day.

The wolf stepped back slightly, plopped back onto its haunches, and tilted its head at her. Kryda adjusted herself into a more upright position and studied the wolf in return. He was magnificent. His bright silver fur glimmered in the light filtering through the trees, and his blue eyes were deep and cool. Kryda thought briefly of a trip she had taken with her father once, to the snowy lands far to the north. She had seen blue like that in the frozen waters there—deep and cold, and yet shimmering with sunlight.

The wolf lowered its head in a quaint bow. As it did so, a howl of wind ruffled the wolf's fur, but left the surrounding trees completely still. The wind smelled faintly of snow and ice, and it gave Kryda a chill in spite of the beam of warm sunlight she was sitting in.

You have done well, young dwarf. I look forward to our adventures. A deep voice echoed, everywhere at once; inside and outside of her head, reverberating through every tree and up from the ground where she sat. Before Kryda could recover enough to react, the wolf trotted back into the trees, and melted into the forest between one blink and the next.

* * *

CHAPTER 2

Kryda blinked rapidly, the embers of her fire in the forest coming back into focus. She was suddenly aware of three things: one, she was actually awake now; two, the sun was coming up; and three, she was clearly losing her mind. She hoped it wasn't something she ate, although that at least would mean it would probably go away. She didn't want to think of the alternative. Her stomach growled, and she was reminded that her meager meal of the night before wouldn't possibly be enough to sustain her for a day's journey. She needed to hunt.

Shaking off the remaining fogginess of sleep, and thoughts of that strange vision, Kryda stamped out her fire and set out for a hunt, a piece of jerky dangling from her mouth like a gnomish cigar. She *really* wanted to head east towards the promise of some good gnomish ale, but hunting would be more fruitful to the north, so she compromised and made her way northeast. If she brought back enough game, she'd be well supplied enough to head due east tomorrow.

The rain had made the ground soft and pliant, forcing Kryda to plod forward as her boots were sucked into the mud. *At least,* she thought, *I can stop worryin' about leavin' any tracks.* The air smelled faintly of decaying underbrush, with the promise of fresh growth to follow, as is typical after a good rain. But as she continued along, Kryda became more and more aware of an unusual rotten sweetness in the breeze that put her on edge.

Pushing on, she noticed other strange changes in her surroundings. The forest was eerily quiet, and everything toward the north seemed…sickly. Not dying, exactly—still strong, but as if its aim was no longer to grow and thrive but to choke out all other life. Her curiosity trumped her hunger, and she veered north, kneeling to observe the ground and vegetation as she went.

There were still many plants here which she recognised as medicinal, but she did not dare try to pluck any for future use. They just didn't *feel* right. When she came to a stream, she didn't care to drink from it, either; but she noticed one plant that looked healthier than the rest. Kryda didn't recognise it. It was deep red, and the soil around it seemed…cleaner somehow, as if the heart-shaped plant were pumping new strength into the soil. She gently tugged a leaf from the plant, pressing it carefully between her fingers. She tucked it into her bag for future study, and pressed onward.

A branch snapped nearby, and Kryda whirled around, pulling out her skinning knife to brace for danger. Slipping on the wet slope, she lost her grip on her knife, and it tumbled into the stream. Swearing colorfully, she looked back up to see an enormous boar standing in front of her, snorting threateningly as it lowered its head, sharp tusks at the ready.

There was a strange, malevolent intelligence in its look as it stared her down with no fear, looking almost regal. Kryda tried to back slowly toward the stream to retrieve her blade, but the moment she moved, the beast charged. Rolling hastily to the side, she successfully evaded its attack, but the boar was now positioned directly between her and the knife. Gritting her teeth, she pulled her pickaxe from her belt. It wouldn't be the cleanest kill, but she had no other choice.

The beast turned to charge her again, but it slipped on the slope just as she had done, and Kryda quickly scrambled to regain higher ground and a more solid footing. She wanted to try and lead the boar away from the stream, onto sturdier ground, before she attempted to kill it. Now sure of her position, she once again began to back away slowly. Strangely enough, the boar did not attempt to charge her again, as if it knew she had regained the advantage. Its beady eyes followed her knowingly as she disappeared back into the foliage.

It seemed wrong that the boar was hunting *her*, wrong like everything else in this strange, murky patch of forest. She ducked quickly behind a tree and listened intently, not only for the beast, but for anything else that might help or hinder her. All she could hear above the pounding of her heartbeat in her ears was the wet snuffling of the boar as it ambled along, following her scent. There was no doubt left in Kryda's mind. It *was* hunting her.

Kryda could neither hear nor see any other woodland animals—no birds, deer or even squirrels. As she listened to the beast snuffle closer to the tree that sheltered her, she closed her eyes and took a deep breath, preparing herself for the attack. The moment her eyelids flicked shut, another vision flashed in her mind.

She saw the wolf from her earlier dream. High above it, crouched in a tree,

CHAPTER 2

a young man stared intently down at it, reaching slowly for the sling tucked into his belt. She blinked, and suddenly she saw *herself*. She had just enough time to realize that she was seeing through the eyes of the wolf before it leaped to attack her; no, it did not leap *at* her, it leapt *into* her. Kryda gasped, reeling from her vision but her thoughts were cut short when the beast raised its head, finally spotting its prey and charged. Kryda dodged and the boar hit the tree instead. With a swift spin, she positioned herself behind the creature and it let out an angry squeal as her pickaxe bit deep into its hindquarters.

Kryda leaped back and tightened her grip on her pickaxe as she prepared for the beast to retaliate. But it did not move; it was frozen, as if rooted to the spot. Thick, dark blood oozed slowly from the wound in its haunch, thicker than Kryda had ever seen blood run before. She stared, shocked, as the black blood rippled—and then began to seep back into the cut as if irresistibly drawn by something inside the beast. The boar shook its head and snorted, trembling violently, pawing at the muddy soil.

Kryda stared, her mouth hanging open. *That doesnae bode well for tryin' to kill it,* she thought grimly. She lowered her pickaxe, crouching low and creeping towards the wounded boar for a better look. The moment she moved, the boar's head snapped back up, its beady gaze boring directly into hers. For a brief second, its eyes looked *right*—the fearful, wild eyes of a wounded animal.

It's badly ill, Kryda realized, a shock of horror curling her toes, *and it* knows *it.* She realized then that she *must* kill the beast—not for food, not to defend herself, but to put it to rest. She tightened her grip on her pickaxe, flooded with pity. *I'm sorry.*

3

Chapter 3

The Beast Slayer

"Mother, I'm going out now. I'll be back for lunch," Marcus called, shouting across their home as he strapped a hunting knife to his ankle, his practiced, callous fingers tightening the leather thongs for what must have been the thousandth time.

"Please do be careful, dear," his mother replied anxiously, appearing in the doorway. Marcus grinned, tossing a lock of dark hair out of his eyes, and looked up at her.

"Always, mother," he promised, tucking his sling into his belt and standing to press a quick kiss to his mother's cheek. She reached up to pat his cheek fondly, smiling back at her tall son. Marcus embraced her, hugging her tightly, then strode towards the entrance of their home.

Pausing at the doorway, he fingered the necklace in the pouch on his belt and sighed. "Don't worry, Angela," he murmured. "I'll make the forest safe again, my love." Pulling the precious necklace from the pouch, he kissed the shell strung on it and gazed at it for a long, heavy moment, then tied it around his wrist and sighed heavily. He was supposed to marry her, before the illness took her. He had done everything he could, summoning healers from places he barely knew of, grasping at every last straw—but every last healer had been stumped. And she was only the first to fall ill.

Soon, hunters were collapsing upon their return from the woods. Then, villagers that had hardly strayed beyond the village walls just to gather berries and herbs also fell deathly sick. Eventually, the hunters were able to discover the source of the illness—a huge, diseased boar, spreading sickness throughout the forest. At first, heavily armed search parties were sent out to comb the woods in hopes of slaying the beast that carried the disease. But as more fell ill with every venture into the corrupted land, panic seized the village, and fewer and fewer soldiers and hunters were bold enough to venture past the wall. And now there was no one left but Marcus.

Turning back to his mother, Marcus forced his features into a reassuring smile, before heading out for yet another fruitless hunt. Although he was alone, Marcus didn't fear the beast, nor the scourge it carried. He had mastered the art of hunting from the treetops, which was much less of a risk than patrolling through the woods with only a spear, never sure from which direction the beast might come. Watching from above, he could also ascertain which animals had been corrupted by the sickness, and which remained miraculously healthy.

As the only hunter brave enough to go back into the woods, he was also the only remaining source of fresh game for the village. He rarely had time to worry about the village scourge at all anymore—Marcus would like nothing better than to bring the terrible beast down himself, but if anything were to happen to him, there would be no one left to look after his mother. So he had made a promise to himself—if he were ever to come upon the beast, it would be by chance alone. Feeding his people would have to come first. He took up his bow and quiver and strode out the door.

* * *

CHAPTER 3

Marcus slung his bow and quiver over his shoulder as he strode towards the old willow at the edge of the village. The tree had always given him comfort, ever since he was a child. It was where he had shared his first kiss with his fiancee, and was now the safest way for him to exit the village. He hefted himself up its ancient trunk, climbing to a vantage point that gave him a line of sight to the guards at the gate and whistling sharply.

"I'm going out," he called, and was met with terse nods from the guards.

"Good luck," one called back, his voice grim. Marcus paid the guard no heed, and swung himself out onto the farthest-reaching branch of the willow. The first few trees on the outer edge of the village were close enough together that he could jump from one branch to another, if he moved carefully. Where they had grown too far apart, Marcus had set up a network of rope bridges between the trees, so that he could stay above ground.

He had just begun his trek over the first of these bridges when a grey flash of movement appeared at the corner of his eye. He quickly whirled to face it, but there was nothing there, and no possible hiding place for anything that might have been there. For a moment, he thought it was merely a trick of the light, but a strange instinct compelled him to follow it.

His network of bridges would get him there efficiently enough, but he could move faster on land. Carefully surveying the surrounding area to ensure it was safe, he decided to take the risk and cross the clearing on the ground. Sliding quickly down the branch of the tree, he knelt down to inspect the earth.

The familiar signs of the beast's passing were there—sickly vegetation and a thick black slime—but they were old. However, as he looked up to follow the trail, he noticed something much stranger. In the place where he thought he'd seen movement, the vegetation seemed to be healthier—almost too healthy, too bright, as if it were glowing.

One plant in particular caught his attention. He didn't know all that much about healing herbs, but his mother had used this one on him often, whenever he'd gotten a cut and been foolish enough to ignore it until it was swollen with pus. She would reopen the cut, drain as much of the fluid as she could, and then make a poultice of this very plant to draw out the rest of the poison.

He'd also seen the village healer use it on a friend of his, who'd made the mistake of bothering a venomous snake. *Ezra might like to have this*, Marcus mused, carefully uprooting the plant and placing it in his satchel. *I'm sure her stock of herbs is not as plentiful as it used to be.*

Resuming his search for the mysterious creature, Marcus finally spotted some sort of tracks, heading south, but the earth was too muddy for the animal to have left a clear print, so he could not yet identify it. Fortunately, his network of rope bridges also wove southward, so he could resume his search from the trees. Climbing back up, he crept along the bridges, moving as slowly as possible so as not to spook the animal should it appear once again.

Hearing a brief rustle in the foliage below him, Marcus froze and peered into the bushes. To his surprise, the creature was a very large wolf—the biggest he'd ever seen. Holding his breath, Marcus stared down at the wolf, reaching slowly for an arrow to nock in his bow. Just as his fingers brushed the shaft's feather, the wolf turned and looked directly at him, its blue eyes boring deep into his for a brief moment before it disappeared back into the woods.

Cursing under his breath, Marcus swung down from the trees without a second thought and plunged into the woods after it. He crashed heedlessly forward, paying no mind to his surroundings. He stumbled up a small rise, and as he reached the top, he saw the wolf. It was crouched low to the ground, its hackles raised, growling deep and low—so low that Marcus almost fancied the earth trembling beneath his feet. But it was not growling at him.

The bushes in front of the wolf rustled violently, branches snapping under a heavy weight. Two long, gleaming tusks emerged slowly from the wreckage, followed by the lowered, malevolent head of the monstrous boar. Marcus swallowed thickly, reaching once again to nock an arrow—but this time with nothing more than a burning desire to save the great grey wolf from the horrible beast.

The wolf backed slowly away from the boar, still growling, its snow-white fangs gleaming in the scattered rays of sun that filtered through the trees. As it backed away, Marcus spotted yet another rustle of movement from the

CHAPTER 3

trees between the two threatening creatures.

The small figure of a little girl stepped out from the forest, taking slow but sure steps towards the boar. The beast snarled, thick saliva drooling uncontrollably from its lips, but the child was undeterred. Marcus glanced back to where the wolf had been, but it had vanished entirely into the forest. For the first time in years, a stab of terror clutched Marcus' heart, and his fingers went involuntarily to the shell necklace around his wrist. He had been unable to save the girl he loved, but all he knew now was that he had to rescue this one before the beast struck.

If he wounded the boar now, he knew with certainty that it would charge and kill the child—he had no choice but to stay his hand. He needed to get closer. Heart pounding, Marcus began to creep cautiously towards the cloaked child, moving stealthily from tree to tree, trying to get close enough that he could whisper to her. With every step, the icy grip of terror closed more tightly around his thrumming heart—one misstep, one cracked twig, and both he and the young girl would have no chance of escape.

He was *so* close now, but he feared that one word from his lips to grab her attention would alert the beast as well. He pressed his back up against the tree that sheltered him, eyes closed, breathing deeply, preparing himself to make a move. After a few short seconds, he was ready to make his move. He searched for any opening in the trees that he could pull her through to safety, but he saw none. There was nothing left for him to do but face the beast head-on and hope the girl would take her opportunity to flee. He closed his eyes, gritted his teeth, and whispered a single word.

"Angela..."

* * *

A heavy, calloused hand slammed into Marcus' chest, knocking the breath from his lungs in a hiss and pressing him back into the tree. His hand scrambled for his hunting knife, but the hand quickly seized his wrist in an iron grip. He stared wide-eyed at his assailant—it was the child, except she wasn't a child. The cloaked figure who he'd taken to be a little girl was, in fact, a dwarf woman, her deep blue eyes frowning into his with no sign of fear.

"Shhh!" she hissed, turning once again to face the boar. "Ye'll startle 'im!"

Marcus' shocked gaze flicked between the woman and the beast. She was staring at it intently, and the beast was looking right back. Up close, Marcus could see that it barely even looked like it should be *alive*, let alone terrorizing his entire village. Its body was criss-crossed with open wounds, oozing the same thick black slime he had usually used to track the beast. *Is that its blood!?* Marcus thought incredulously. The hot black liquid rippled along the beast's flanks as if it had a life of its own, thick dark wisps of smoke rising from its foul surface as it pulsed in and out of the jagged cuts in the boar's flesh.

The dwarf woman released her hold on Marcus, taking a cautious step towards the beast. It snorted, black ooze spurting from its nostrils, then shook its head and charged, swinging its heavy head to gore her with its tusks. The woman leapt to the side, moving faster than the beast could, given its horribly wounded state, and drew a weapon from her belt, crouching in a defensive position and waiting for the beast to charge her again.

Marcus fumbled for his bow. "Listen," he called, his voice hoarse. "I can help you."

Neither the boar nor the woman seemed to take any notice of him, as they circled one another, each waiting for the other to make a move. Marcus nocked an arrow and pulled the string taut, waiting for the beast to make a move, but the two were so close together that he was fearful of shooting the dwarf woman instead. The woman began to speak, and at first Marcus thought she would accept his offer of help, but she was speaking to the boar, murmuring softly in a language Marcus didn't understand.

The beast growled and charged again, but the dwarf woman was ready. She swung the flat side of her weapon—no, not a sword or a club, a *pickaxe*—toward the beast's head. A horrible *snap* echoed through the forest as it connected with one of the beast's tusks, spraying fragments of bone and marrow. The force of the blow sent the woman stumbling backwards, and

CHAPTER 3

Marcus saw his chance.

The arrow buried itself deep in the flesh of the beast's shoulder, and it screamed in pain and rage, but did not pause. Not seeing Marcus, it charged the woman again, but she hadn't yet recovered, and Marcus felt a heavy stone drop in his stomach as he realized she was doomed, and he had doomed her.

The woman rolled swiftly to avoid the brunt of the charge, but the boar's remaining tusk plunged deep into her thigh. She swore violently in pain, lashing out with her pickaxe and catching its point on the beast's front leg, tearing flesh and tendons away from its bone. The boar stumbled forward, directly into a tree, its bloodied tusk sinking into the bark and catching the dwarf's pickaxe torn from her grasp by the force of its momentum.

Hands trembling, Marcus nocked another arrow as the woman snatched up her pickaxe, struggling to her feet as hot red blood streamed down her wounded thigh. The boar squealed with fury, freeing itself from the tree. Perhaps sensing his intent, the dwarf glanced back at Marcus just as he released the arrow.

"NO!" she cried.

The arrow found its mark, ripping deep into the boar's neck, slicing through tendons and arteries and bursting through the other side in a spray of black gore. The beast remained standing, stock-still for a few brief, terrifying seconds, before collapsing heavily to the ground, ooze pulsing from the wound.

Marcus sank to his knees in relief, his bow slipping from his grasp as he released a sob of relief. He was only distantly aware of a storm of curses as the woman limped towards him, before her sturdy hand seized him by the collar and hauled him off the ground.

"What are ye, crazy!?" she demanded. "What the hell did ye do that for?"

Marcus scrambled for his footing, trying to loosen the grip on his collar. "What the hell were *you* doing!?" he spat back. "That thing has been terrorizing my village for months, and you were trying to *befriend* it!?"

"AYE!"

Stunned by the blunt reply, Marcus let himself go limp, and the woman released her grip on his collar and turned away, looking back towards the fallen boar. She turned back to Marcus, a deep, thoughtful sadness in her mesmerizing blue gaze.

"Look there," she continued, more calmly this time. "D'ya see? This is no normal beast. It's full of evil."

"I know," he replied irritably, dusting himself off and retrieving his bow. "That's why I've been trying to kill the fucking thing."

"Shhh! Calm down. It's feedin' on your fear and anger," she hissed.

"It's dead," he replied, but she seemed so certain that he automatically pulled another arrow from his quiver, nocked it, and pushed past the woman to get a better look at the downed boar.

"No," she said calmly. "There's an evil controlling it. The boar is still alive, trapped in there, unable to control the evil growing inside. It's just a vessel."

Marcus cautiously approached the boar, which remained deathly still, but began to draw the arrow back just in case. "How do you know all this?"

For the first time, her voice wavered. "Well, I just...feel it. The boar, I mean. It's still in there."

Marcus glanced back at her questioningly, and as he did so, he heard a rustling behind him. He whirled back to face the boar, only to find the beast was, as the dwarf woman had said, still most certainly alive. The flesh around his arrow sizzled with greasy black smoke, sealing itself around the wound, the blood pulsating instead of dripping. Marcus stumbled backward and fired his bow—but in his shock, it thudded uselessly into the earth just in front of the beast's shredded leg. And then the boar charged him.

Marcus closed his eyes and readied himself for death. He had been so close, so *close* to avenging Angela, to saving his village, from a horror that no one understood, least of all himself—and he had failed.

But then he heard her.

Singing.

His eyes flew open to the most astonishing sight he had ever witnessed. The dwarf woman was circling the beast cautiously, one hand extended, palm outward. And she was singing softly. The beast snorted, shaking its head violently, reopening the wound in its neck. The hot black ooze was pouring out, but it was no longer clinging to the boar as it once had. It was dripping,

CHAPTER 3

spattering against the ground, seeping into the earth.

Marcus stared in wonder as the woman's extended hand came closer and closer to the beast's head. The pickaxe in her other hand clattered to the ground as she advanced, slowly, confidently. It almost seemed like there was a soft, gentle light emanating from her palm, glowing in contrast to the darkness surrounding the beast.

Beauty, in the face of evil.

The beast backed away as the woman advanced, its head lowering, stumbling on its wounded leg. Black blood was pouring from it in great, frantic pulses now, and Marcus was faintly reminded of sailors leaping off the side of a sinking ship. The woman slowly began to lower her hand towards the great head of the beast as the blood gushed from it in fountains.

The beast let out one great, final snort that was almost a gasp, as its chin settled against the ground. Its eyes closed as the woman's palm settled gently against the top of its head. Its breathing slowed, and its color started to change, as the last of the black slime and smoke seeped into the earth, withering the plants as it went.

The dwarf started to stroke the beast, and Marcus saw that wherever her hand touched, the skin of the beast became healed and bright. The woman smiled, radiantly. She looked up at Marcus.

"C'mere, lad."

Marcus stood, tremblingly, and moved towards the woman and the boar. He paused briefly, afraid it would rise once again to strike. The woman glared at him and motioned impatiently for him to come and stand beside her. Marcus approached reluctantly and stood silently beside her, watching her stroke the beast's head.

Before Marcus could react, the woman once again grasped his wrist with her other hand and placed his palm upon the animal as well. The beast heaved a great sigh, and for the first time, Marcus could see the thing in front of him as a wounded animal in need of help, and not the monster he'd been chasing for so long.

Even as that thought tugged at his mind, the beast changed further. It began to shrink, smaller and smaller, until the terrifying monstrosity in front of him was no more than a youngling boar, trembling, frail and vulnerable, with a hunter's arrow through its neck, bright red blood trickling from the wound. There was still one great, pulsating blob of darkness right where the path to its heart was, but it seemed that whatever the woman had done to the animal had sealed it there, unable to escape. The boar grunted in pain as more blood spilled from its neck, and the heaving dark mass under its skin struggled against its confinement.

"I know, little one," the dwarf woman murmured, not to Marcus, but to the boar. She sighed heavily and bent down to retrieve her pickaxe. "It'll be better soon. I promise." She lifted the pickaxe high above her head, then brought it down perfectly in the center of the darkness where the boar's heart should have been.

The youngling died instantly, but whatever was inside it released a shriek like Marcus had never heard before, and the withered grasses around it hissed and smoked, as if whatever had been in control of the animal resented the loss of its vessel and its territory. As the last echoes of the shriek died away, silence once again descended over the forest.

Her work done, the dwarven woman sat back heavily on the ground with a sigh, dropping her pickaxe. She looked incredibly exhausted, but unnaturally peaceful—there was no regret in the killing, but certainly no celebration, either.

* * *

Marcus was the first to break the silence. "Well," he said, offering a hand to help her up, "we need to get you back to the village, and soon."

The woman waved him away dismissively, but when she tried to stand, she winced in pain and collapsed. Marcus shot her a pointed look and once again extended his hand, and this time she accepted his help, glaring resentfully at the wound in her thigh. He threw an arm around her shoulders to help her walk.

CHAPTER 3

"It's just a scratch. I'll be fine," she insisted, trying to shrug him off, but her ordeal had exhausted her, and she couldn't loosen his grip.

"I've seen this kind of 'scratch' many times," Marcus told her grimly, "and I've rarely seen anyone recover. We need to get you to the healer in case some of the poison remains and takes hold. I just hope we can get back in time."

"Well…thanks. Me name's Kryda, by the way," she replied dryly. Marcus couldn't help but smile wryly at her dismissive air. He dipped his head by way of introduction.

"Marcus," he replied, reaching down to pick up his bag and bow. As he did so, the plant he'd collected earlier tumbled out of the satchel.

"What's tha'?" she asked.

"Ah, just a medicinal plant I collected earlier today." He paused briefly. "Actually, that might help you. I'm pretty sure it's used to draw out poison. I don't know what our healer has been using on this particular poison, but it couldn't hurt to try…"

"Pretty sure?" she snorted. "I'm pretty sure it could do more harm than good if ye don't know what yer doin' with it." She shoved against him roughly, knocking the wind out of him and freeing herself from his grasp as her broad shoulder collided with his chest. He hadn't expected her to be quite so strong, even though he knew that dwarves were much sturdier than humans. She limped away so quickly that Marcus had to jog a few steps to catch up.

"Look, I'm no expert in herbs, but I've had this one used on me enough times to be confident about its basic use. I can't guarantee that it'll work on your wound, but I *can* guarantee that it won't *kill* you, which, by the way, the poison very well could," he replied irritably.

Kryda paused and turned to look at him. She really did look a bit like a child, staring up at him like that, but her eyes were far too full of guarded mysteries to be the innocent gaze of a child. She sighed and sat obstinately back down on the ground.

"Fine, then, if you're so eager to play healer, let's get on wit' it," she grumbled. Marcus grinned at his victory and knelt beside her, awkwardly wrapping the leaves around the wound.

"I'll need to roll your trousers up to hold them in place," he said, hesitantly.

"If yer so sure ye must," she replied, winking teasingly at him. Marcus blushed beet red, carefully cutting the lower leg of her trousers with his knife and folding it neatly up over the leaves, securing them tightly. Kryda grunted.

"Right, let's get on then, back to this healer o' yers." She gruffly extended her hand, shooting him a pointed glance when he paused in confusion.

"Oh. Right." Marcus flashed her an apologetic smile and seized her arm, helping her back to her feet. She tottered forward on her newly bandaged leg, then turned and glared at him.

"Well? I know you came from this direction, but I don't actually know where you came from! Why're you followin' me?"

Choking back a sigh, Marcus led the irritable magic dwarf back to his village.

CHAPTER 3

4

Chapter 4

The Villagers

As they approached the village gates, Kryda quickly noticed that the bulk of its inhabitants were all gathered in the square, absorbed in anxious conversation. Marcus' mother spotted them and came rushing to meet him.

"Marcus! Oh, thank the gods you're alright! We heard a terrible noise and I was afraid you weren't coming home." She threw her arms around him and embraced him fiercely, as the rest of the village began crowding around them, babbling multitudes of questions.

Kryda was slowly pushed back from the circle, which suited her just fine. She stood off to the side as the whole village fawned over Marcus, asking him what he'd seen out in the forest, if he knew what that dreadful sound was. Kryda touched one hand to her temple, feeling lightheaded...*it must be the effects of the poison*, she thought.

She watched the crowd, waiting for Marcus to calm them down so that he could actually get a word in edgewise, when she noticed one woman staring intently at her. *She must be the healer Marcus spoke about*, Kryda thought. The woman studied her for a few more heartbeats, nodded briefly to Kryda and shuffled away toward a small hut nearly lost in ivy and blossoms.

Definitely the healer, Kryda thought wryly. She looked back at Marcus, who was searching for her over the heads of the crowd. Catching his eye, she nodded towards the healer's hut. He nodded back and resumed the ordeal of facing down the villagers, clearly exasperated by their unceasing flow of questions.

Kryda grinned at his misfortune and hobbled towards the healer's hut as quickly as she could with the poison coursing through her system, slowing her down. She rapped heavily on the door.

"Come in," a gentle voice called. Kryda pushed the door open to see the old woman pulling a pot of tea out of the stove, using a broad leaf to safely grip the sizzling handle. She poured a cup for Kryda, her hand trembling, but somehow managing to spill not a single drop.

"Yer not 'aving any, then?" Kryda asked, noticing that there was no cup for the healer herself.

"Oh, no," laughed the old woman. "I've had more than my fair share of *that* tea." She chuckled pleasantly as she turned to prepare a fresh pot with different herbs. "I thought it would be Marcus I'd be treating when the gods impressed upon me to make this tea today," she mused. "Glad it wasn't. No offense, dear, it's no good that you've been afflicted either, but your body will handle it much better than his would. Sturdy folk, your people are. Also, he's a terrible whiner when it comes to drinking what's good for him." She shot Kryda a wry look and smiled warmly. "Men usually are."

Kryda smiled in return and accepted the tea, sipping it gratefully, then promptly spitting it all over the woman's apron.

"Ugh! This is bloody vile!" she protested. The old woman peered sternly at her over her glasses. "Ah, sorry," Kryda backtracked. "What the he—what's in this tea?"

"You really don't want to know," the woman replied matter-of-factly. "It's much better if you just plug your nose and drink it all up as quick as you can. The other tea I have here is much more pleasant. You can wash it down with that, if you behave."

Kryda hated being told what to do like that, but the woman reminded her of her Gran so she nodded meekly and did as she was instructed. The moment she gulped down the last swallow of the vile brew and set the empty cup down on the table, a fresh cup of hot, delicious-smelling tea was pressed into her hand. It did taste much better, but it was far too hot to wash down the taste of the other one quickly, and Kryda made some unpleasant faces as the old woman sat down beside her to examine her leg.

"What made you decide to use this plant?" she inquired. Midway through a sip of delicious tea, Kryda swallowed hastily, still trying to wash out the taste of the first cup.

"Marcus 'ad picked it before 'e found me. I think 'e'd planned to give it to ye, and said 'e thought it migh' bring out some of the poison."

"Well, he wasn't wrong," she said matter-of-factly, "and it probably made my job a bit easier. However, this plant is not strong enough for the poison in your system. The tea I gave you will slow your circulation, and therefore the spread of the poison, but it will not cure you. I will have to remove some of the infected tissue here, but I'm afraid I cannot put you to sleep to do it. The fact is, it will be very painful."

Kryda nodded, prepared to accept whatever was necessary to regain the use of her leg. The healer peered at Kryda over her glasses, taking a handful of stringy roots from a nearby jar and passing them to Kryda. "Chew on these, dear. They will help with the pain and give you something to focus on. Are you ready?"

Kryda nodded again, slightly more shakily this time. The healer returned to the fire and drew out a red-hot knife. Kryda stared at it, eyes wide, and drew in a deep breath.

"If anyone can ever be ready for something like this, then aye, I guess I am."

Her teeth clamped down hard on the roots.

* * *

The entire town stood silent as Kryda's shrieks rang out from the healer's hut.

CHAPTER 4

Marcus was the first to move, since he was the only one who knew who was in the hut, and what she was being treated for. He had told the village what had become of the beast, but he hadn't gotten to the part about Kryda being infected. It didn't take the villagers long to figure it out, though. They'd seen it before.

Some of the villagers followed slowly after Marcus, expecting to find that they had lost another poor soul. Marcus' mother was right behind him, peeking over his shoulder as she lay a hand there to comfort him, not knowing who she would see lying on the table.

The fierce-eyed dwarf woman on the healer's table had just removed the chewn-up piece of bark from her mouth, grunting in pain as the healer tightened a bandage around her thigh. Marcus sighed in relief, his mother glancing curiously between the dwarf woman and her son.

"Are you—is she—going to be okay?" Marcus ventured, unsure who he should be directing the question to.

"She'll need to rest—" began the healer, but Kryda waved her away, cutting her off.

"I'm fine!" Kryda hopped off the table, seizing it briefly to steady herself, but then standing tall, swaying only slightly on her injured leg. Marcus reached out to lend her a hand, but she waved him away as well.

"I may be a bit unsteady for now, but I can feel the poison is gone." She closed her eyes tightly for a moment, testing her strength, but found herself still weakened by the tea the woman had given her. "Have ye got another tea or sumit' teh fix me from the last one?" she asked.

The villagers had caught up with Marcus and his mother, and were now staring at the dwarf woman in shock. She shouldn't even be conscious, let alone *standing*.

The healer gave Kryda a hard look, but the old woman recognized the stubbornness in the young dwarf—just like herself, when she was young. Her glare melted into an indulgent smile, and she rummaged through her herbs, sprinkling something sweet-smelling in the boiling cauldron.

Knowing that her legs were still too weak to allow her to walk for very long, she leaned against the table while she waited, the curious gazes of dozens of villagers boring into her broad back as she smirked.

After a few minutes of heavy silence, the old woman scooped some of the fresh tea into a metal funnel that spiraled around at the end. It was a strange contraption, and Kryda wasn't sure why she would bother with it until she took a tentative sip of the tea and found that it was already cool enough to drink!

She downed the tea quickly, feeling her strength returning almost immediately. The healer watched as the colour returned to her face and the fog of pain began to lift from her eyes. Satisfied that the young dwarf would indeed recover, she nodded briefly to Kryda and then turned to the wide-eyed crowd that had gathered.

"She's FINE!" the healer bellowed. "Now, out of my house, all of you!" She shooed them impatiently, smiling at the dwarf, before disappearing into the back room.

***

The villagers had spilled from the healer's hut and back into the sun, but they hadn't exactly dispersed. They crowded around Marcus and Kryda, but Marcus' mother shooed them away and escorted the two back to her home.

"So sorry about all that, dear," she told Kryda apologetically. "We don't normally get a lot of excitement around here. The whole business with the beast was not the good kind, but then there was you! Everyone is just dying to know how you two defeated the thing. I'm sure you know we've been after it for quite some time now. How DID you do it?"

"Och, ye jus' needed the right bait." Kryda gestured to herself, chuckling deep in her chest as she uncorked her wineskin with a flourish—then grimaced as she upended it and found it empty.

Marcus' mother shot Kryda a glance that said she was less than impressed with the joke. "People often do not return from the forest, dear, and even when they do, not even Ezra—bless her heart—can do anything for them,"

CHAPTER 4

she sighed.

Marcus leaned down to whisper in Kryda's ear. "That's the healer."

"I gathered tha'." Kryda rolled her eyes and lifted her wineskin in a silent plea. Marcus flashed her a crooked grin and got up to fetch some wine from the shelf while he described their adventure to his mother—with the occasional interjection from Kryda. By the time he had finished, Kryda was waving an empty wine bottle in his direction.

"Sorry, Kryda, that's all we've got. We can head over to the tavern. though, if you'd like."

"Aye, I could use another bottle, an' I suppose I should be findin' me a place ta sleep for the night. I should be gettin' on early in the mornin'." Kryda ran her hand through her hair nervously, suddenly reminded of the urgency of her travels. She knew she wasn't nearly far enough away from her own village just yet. She took a quick peek into her money pouch and winced.

"Well, you don't have to stay at the tavern if you don't want to. After we get a drink or two, of course you can come back here for the night."

Kryda thought for a moment, then nodded her assent. "Alright," she said, her head already filling with dreams of gnomish wine. "Let's go, then!"

* * *

Unfortunately for Kryda, the tavern did not offer gnomish wine, but she soon forgot her disappointment as she spent the evening drinking and talking with Marcus. She learned more about the struggles they'd had in the village because of the possessed boar. Some other people from the village often came by to thank the two for ridding them of the beast, and Marcus insisted every time that it was all Kryda's doing.

Marcus asked Kryda all about her own home, and learned readily of the dwarven village to the south and their way of life, as well as some stories of their past. Kryda told one tale in particular that really captured Marcus' attention, as well as that of the rest of the tavern, since she had drunkenly decided to tell most of it from atop the table.

She spoke of the brave dwarven warriors that used to inhabit ten times the area around their current village, and of their alliances with the creatures of the land. Marcus was particularly intrigued when Kryda spoke of her great-great-grandmother and her wolf companion with blue eyes. He wondered about his own vision of a blue-eyed wolf, but was so enthralled by Kryda's story that he didn't interrupt.

She continued on, rambling about a nearby clan who joined forces with her people all those years ago, a clan led by a valiant dwarven warrior and his panther. Side by side, the Wolf clan and the Panther clan fought back the goblins and orcs. The two clans thereafter lived in close relations, until the Drow clans split them from either side and drove them both back to the core of their cities.

The Wolf clan built a fallback shelter with artificial mountains, a stronghold which would later become Kryda's small secluded village. The Wolf clan dwarves never heard from the Panther clan again, and therefore assumed that they were wiped out, but travelers have since told stories of catching glimpses of the Panther's spirit, declaring that the Panther clan may yet rise once again.

By the time Kryda finished her story, every occupant of the tavern had their eyes on her. When it was clear that she was finished, the silence erupted into a great drunken cheer. The crowd lifted Kryda off the table, passing her around the tavern atop the throng of people, with shouts of "Kryda! Beast Slayer!" and the like.

Marcus remained silent, smiling at the crowd's excitement. The village hadn't been in such high spirits in ages, and it was all thanks to this strange traveling dwarf. He wondered about the Panther clan. He knew his people had been here for generations, so they must have known something about the dwarves, but he had never heard Kryda's story before. Perhaps they were just some legend among her people. He knew very well how stories could become inflated over generations.

When the excitement finally died down, Marcus made his way through the crowd towards Kryda and pulled the drunken dwarf aside. "It's late, Kryda.

CHAPTER 4

We should head back home."

Kryda blinked owlishly at him, swaying on her feet. Marcus was briefly concerned that her leg was bothering her again, but after a glance over to the wide-eyed bartender and an entire wagon's worth of empty ale bottles, Marcus was reassured that it was a miracle she was standing at all.

"Aye, I suppose it's about time to be gettin' some sleep. Lemme jus' git meh some brew fer tha road," she mumbled, sloppily refilling her wineskin and loudly requesting a couple of extra bottles of ale. "It's actually not bad…fer human ale, that is!" She slapped Marcus on the shoulder, hard, as she said it, and he rubbed his arm with a grin.

* * *

When they returned to the house, Marcus' mother had already made up the couch for her son to sleep on—so Kryda could have his bed for the night—and a small fire was glowing in their little hearth. But before Marcus could open his mouth to speak, the dwarf flopped straight onto the couch with a grin and a sigh. "Thanks fer that evenin' Marcus. I had a great time, I did! Yer people are good people." She smirked briefly, but then her expression sank slowly into a concerned frown, and she fell silent for a moment.

"They all think I'm a hero who killed some terrible beast…but it was just a sick animal, really." She sighed and turned away. "D'ye reckon…d'ye think they'll be tellin me story on the trade routes?"

Marcus let out a breath, not sure why she seemed so reluctant to have her tale told. "I think it'd take a miracle to stop 'em," he said wryly.

Kryda glanced back at Marcus, then sighed again and closed her eyes, shifting her position on the couch. "I was afraid o' tha'," she mumbled. "I need tae be takin' more care."

Marcus paused, wondering if it was right for him to be prying information out of the drunken dwarf. But, then again, if he knew what had been troubling her, what drove her away from her home, maybe he could help her. "What do you have to be careful about?" he asked, slowly, calmly.

Kryda opened one eye to look him over before replying. "I ran away," she admitted. "I was supposed tae be Acknowledged yesterday. Tha's the day we choose our jobs, and our partners. I would 'ave been betrothed tae me best friend, Fáelán."

"Why did you leave? You didn't love him?"

"Ach, I loved 'im plenty. He was everythin' to me." Kryda propped herself up on the couch, then reached down to run her fingers over the handle of her pickaxe, and Marcus noticed Fáelán's name carved into the handle. That, along with the look in her eyes, told him that she truly had been in love with the young man.

Kryda shook her head to clear the memories and continued. "But I needed to git out. Me little village has become too comfortable an' soft. Tha' life is nae for me. They would never survive the trials they conquered so many years ago. Someone needs to show them that the world is still out there! All the wonders…and all the dangers. I need to have adventures of me own, and bring the stories back to them someday. They never would 'ave let me go if I'd told 'em. I'm not even full grown yet, in their eyes."

Marcus hesitated. "How old *are* you?"

"I'm only 50. That's our coming of age."

Marcus' eyes widened. *"Only* 50?" he said incredulously. "I knew dwarves aged more slowly, but I didn't realize it was so long as that. 50 years old, and still a child?"

"I'm no child!" Kryda snapped. "In fact, I'm old, by yer standards. When do you humans become adults?"

"That depends on the village." Marcus turned to face the flickering fire, the light playing over his stubbled cheeks. "Here, we celebrate our adulthood when we turn 15. My own ceremony was only a few years ago."

"Less than twenty, still only a lad, and already the wee beginnings of a beard," Kryda teased him. Marcus smiled dryly and ran one hand over his unshaved chin.

"I was supposed to choose a bride soon afterwards," he continued, his voice lowering. "But there was no one here for me…until Angela came from the

CHAPTER 4

village to the east to study with our healer. I fell for her the first time I saw her."

Sensing Marcus' change in tone and his willingness to be fully open with her now that she had been with him, Kryda's eyes softened, and she leaned back on one arm to listen.

"I had fallen from a tree and broken my leg," Marcus recalled, smiling slightly as he stared into the fire, as if he saw her in the dancing flames. "She tended my leg with the help of the healer, then came back to our house every day to make sure that I wasn't putting too much strain on it while it healed. She helped Mother with the chores I should have been doing, and even managed to bring in a few small game animals for us with some traps."

Marcus stood and moved over to the fire, taking up the poker and stirring the embers idly, then leaning it back against the side of the fireplace. "As soon as my leg was healed enough to get down on one knee, I asked for her hand. I was the luckiest man in all the world. We began preparing for our wedding. She went out into the forest to pick a garland of decorative flowers for her hair, and…" Marcus bowed his head and sighed.

"The beast?" Kryda asked, gently, intent upon hearing the rest of his story.

"Yes," Marcus said, grimly. "But she managed to escape, only slightly wounded. The healer treated her with all the skill she had. Angela had such a strong will, we thought…we thought she would easily recover. She was the first to be wounded by the beast, so we didn't yet know how dangerous it was. And at first, she seemed to be getting better. The wound closed, and she was soon up and about again, promising me that there was no need to postpone our wedding."

Marcus bowed his head and squeezed his eyes shut, tears winding their way down his cheeks, their wet trails shimmering in the fire. "She was so strong and beautiful, through all of it. But the evil festering in her wound was too great even for her. I suppose the more she fought it back, the more it was determined to claim her. She died in my arms, just a few days before our wedding."

Marcus sniffled, dragging one arm across his nose. He cleared his throat and straightened back up, turning towards Kryda, who was watching with a deep sympathy in her green eyes. "But that evil will never take anyone again," he said, firmly. "Thanks to you, Kryda."

She huffed, fingers still tracing her pickaxe. "I only did what I felt like I had'ta." She paused. "Ah'm sorry about yer lass, Marcus. I can see what she meant tae ye. She sounds like she was a proper catch."

Marcus smiled faintly at the praise. "Yes. She was." He sighed, shaking his head to clear it. "You should get some rest, Kryda, if you plan to be off first thing tomorrow morning."

"Aye. Thanks again for lettin' me stay 'ere."

"Of course. You did save my whole village, after all. It's the least we could do. And we'll make sure you have whatever you need for the next part of your journey." He smiled fondly at her, a small part of him wishing she didn't have to depart so soon—but he understood that it would be impossible to persuade her otherwise.

"Thank you, Marcus. G'night." The dwarf woman burrowed comfortably into the couch, tugging the blanket up to her chin, and grinned back at him.

"G'night, Kryda," Marcus replied, and headed up the stairs to fall gratefully into his own bed.

***

Kryda awoke to a quiet house, but a bustle outside. Marcus' mother had left her a fresh wash basin nearby, so she scrubbed her face quickly before heading outside to check on the commotion. She had thought it was still very early, but apparently the whole village must have been up and working for some time. They had set up a huge table that seemed to span the entire square, with enough seats and food for everyone.

Nearby, children were laughing and playing, chasing each other with sticks. One of the older girls was chasing a younger boy.

"Come back here, beast! I'll have you for dinner!" she yelled, just as she caught up to the boy. She tackled him, and they tumbled over giggling.

"Ew! No one would want to eat me! I'm just a nasty beast!"

CHAPTER 4

"Yea, you're right! So what should I do with you, then?" A sly grin split the girl's face. "I know! I'll *tickle* you!" The squirming boy squealed and darted out from beneath her, running off in a fit of laughter, and she chased after him. They ran beyond the village wall and out of Kryda's sight, but she could still hear their giggles, and smiled to herself. Marcus saw her there and came over to greet her.

"Wha's all this?" she asked him, gesturing around the square.

"Everyone wanted to see you off. I told them you were planning to leave early, and they just went straight to work preparing this feast for you. It seems a lot of people had started preparations last night while we were at the tavern. They were expecting to hold the feast later tonight, until they saw me getting things ready for you this morning."

The rest of the village was beginning to notice Kryda's emergence, and some were coming to thank her once again, while others worked faster to finish the preparations. The healer—*Ezra*, Kryda reminded herself—and the leader of the village greeted Kryda and showed her to her place in the middle of the table.

"I dunae be needin' all this fuss, really," she protested, but as she sat down, the scent of all that food made her stomach growl. "It do be smellin' heavenly, though." She waited impatiently as the rest of the village found their seats at the table. Ezra and the village leader sat down across from her, and Marcus beside her. As the last few people found their seats, the leader rose to his feet, and the village grew quiet.

"Today, we honour a young dwarf for her bravery in defeating the beast that had taken so many of our people and poisoned our land." Everyone bowed their heads in memory of the lost for a moment, and then the leader continued. "Our scouts have already brought news that the land is producing fresh vegetation again, and the animals are returning!" A cheer rose around the table, but the leader motioned for silence. "This is all thanks to this young woman: Kryda!" The cheer resumed and grew, the villagers stamping their feet and clapping their hands. "Let us feast in her honour this beautiful morning, and forever remember her courage."

With the speech out of the way, everyone began filling their plates. Kryda followed suit, and was pleasantly surprised to find that both the food and ale were even better than what she'd had the night before. But just as she was getting comfortable and the cheering finally began to die down, she felt a tug on her tunic. Kryda looked down to see the little girl she'd seen before, staring up at her nervously.

"Miss Kryda, ma'am...sorry to bother you, but I...I heard that you *sang* to the beast. Is that true?" Kryda glanced quickly at Marcus, who was pointedly ignoring the question. She had hoped he wouldn't tell that part of the story, but of course he had—he was an honest lad, after all. Kryda sighed heavily as she turned back to the girl.

"Well, aye, I—" she began.

"Could you sing for me?? PLEEEEEASE!?" The little girl's eyes lit up like pearls. Kryda glanced at the others around her, hoping that they hadn't overheard the request.

"I dunae sing, little one. Not unless I—" The girl looked so stricken with disappointment that Kryda sighed. She looked around once again, but no one else seemed to be paying any attention. Kryda looked back at the little girl, whose chin was trembling, the beginnings of tears shining at the corners of her eyes.

"Alright! Alright," she whispered to the girl. "I'll sing for ye. Just...keep this a secret between us, alright? I don't like people knowin' about it." The girl's expression brightened again and she bounced excitedly on her toes. Kryda leaned in closer to sing quietly to the girl, her lips hardly moving as she breathed out the song she'd sung to the stricken boar.

Marcus leaned slowly back in his seat to listen, and as he did so, he noticed that the healer was listening as well, her head tilted slightly towards the soft music.

The sounds of the feast seemed to fade away. Kryda had closed her eyes and was singing very softly, like a lullaby. The little girl's eyes fluttered shut as well, and tears started to trickle down her face. When Kryda finally stopped singing, the little girl wiped her tears away and jumped into Kryda's arms.

"Oh, thank you!" she cried, tucking her head into Kryda's shoulder. Alarmed by this sudden display of emotion, Kryda patted the girl's back

CHAPTER 4

gently, shooting Marcus a concerned look.

"Hey, now! Why the tears? It was a happy song, it was! Oh, don't cry, darlin'!"

"It's just," the girl sniffled, "ever since my daddy didn't come back from hunting, my throat always hurt, right here." She pointed to the base of her throat. "I couldn't sing anymore, and I used to all the time. I couldn't cry, either. I tried and tried—and I wanted to—but I just couldn't." Another tear rolled down her cheek, but she was smiling. "But now I can!"

"D'ye think you could remember the song I just sung ye?" Kryda asked, abruptly.

The little girl nodded happily.

"Why don't ye try to sing it now, then?"

The little girl clambered out of Kryda's lap and began to repeat the song that Kryda had sung for her, singing it loudly and clearly so that now the whole village began to stop eating and pay attention. But Kryda was so touched by the little girl that she hardly noticed the audience. When the little one stumbled over a forgotten word, Kryda didn't hesitate to sing along with her, guiding her through the healing song.

When they repeated the verse, Kryda began to sing in harmony, changing one of the lines into a minor key. She had never heard it that way before, since she had always known it to be a joyful song, but in this moment, that one line felt like a perfect tribute to those the village had lost. The little girl grasped for Kryda's hand and held it as their voices reached a crescendo, and slowly let go as their voices quieted and slowed to the end.

When the last notes of their song finally faded away into the wind, the two stood smiling at each other for a moment, before the little girl leaned in to give Kryda another hug. It wasn't until Kryda released the girl that she finally remembered there was an entire village of people surrounding her. She blushed beet red, suddenly embarrassed by her impromptu display, and looked helplessly at Marcus. He shrugged and looked around the table, and Kryda followed his gaze.

It was absolutely quiet, and every villager stood smiling gratefully at Kryda with tears in their eyes. After a long moment, Ezra stepped forward, and the little girl darted forward to wrap her small arms around the healer's leg. The old woman smiled down at the little girl and rested one hand on her head, stroking her hair. The healer looked back at Kryda and nodded slowly.

"Music is the best kind of medicine for the soul. Thank you for your song."

* * *

"Where will you be heading next?" Marcus asked, striding up beside her as she shoved her belongings haphazardly back into her bag. Kryda grinned at him.

"I was plannin' to go get some good ale at the gnome city, but ye know… this stuff's pretty good!" She lifted her wineskin toward him and took a swig. *They would expect me to go there, anyway,* she thought to herself. Then, out loud, "I'll continue North, I s'pose. How far is the nearest town from 'ere in tha' direction?"

"That would be Starting City, about three days due North through the mountain pass, or five days around the pass on the road. There should be a merchant heading through that way in a few days, though, if you'd like to stay awhile and hitch a ride when he comes. The village could use an extra hunter to restock our stores now that the beast is gone," Marcus offered, tentatively.

"I'm no hunter. Minin' be me trade!" Kryda hefted her pickaxe with pride. "I kin feed meself, aye, but I dunae care tae be killin' any more than I be needin'. The mountain pass sounds perfect. Maybe I'll find even somthin' worthwhile on the way." Kryda dug into her pack, pulling out a round, white gem and offering it to Marcus. "Take this fer all yer help, and fer your village. The merchants really seem to like 'em, and they fetch quite a price. I'm not even sure where they come from—I've never found one in the earth, only on the ground in my cave."

Marcus took the gem and inspected it, rolling it between two fingers. "This is a pearl, Kryda. A *huge* pearl. And you found it in a cave?"

CHAPTER 4

"Not just any cave—my secret underwater cave," she replied, grinning slyly. "Me an' Lan are the only ones who ever go down there, 'cause we're the only ones in the village who've learnt to swim. No one else in the village knows where these things come from, and they like em', but never thought the merchants would have much call for em'. They were wrong. The merchants did seem pretty surprised to find them in my little village."

"How much do they usually give you for these?" he asked incredulously.

"Not nearly as much as they're worth," she snorted. "I always figured I was bein' cheated. Of course I didnae know their full value, but I could see the shock in the merchants' eyes before they composed themselves right quick, and I knew they had to be worth more than I was gettin'." Marcus grinned at Kryda's shrewd appraisal of the merchants' greed. "Tha's why I always saved the best ones—like this one—for my journey," she continued. "I expected they'd fetch an even better price in a city that could appreciate 'em."

Marcus nodded, holding the pearl back out to her. "You're right, Kryda. They're worth a fortune, this one especially. I can't accept it."

"Bollocks! I've plenty more. Maybe I'll even find some more up there in the caves in those mountains, too."

Marcus chuckled slightly, and Kryda shot him a questioning look. "I doubt you'll find any more in the mountains," he told her. "These come from clams. From the ocean."

"*Clams?*" she demanded. "Them smelly, slimy sea creatures that fishermen suck right from their shells? Ugh!" Kryda made a face, reaching up to plug her nose, and Marcus laughed aloud.

"Yes, Kryda, those clams. That's why merchants usually expect to buy these from fishermen, not miners," he explained, turning the pearl in his hand and marveling at the perfection of its shape and sheen. "They're mostly ornamental, although I've heard that some people crush them into powder for other uses."

"No! How could anyone think of crushing something so beautiful?" Kryda gasped.

"I don't know," Marcus replied honestly. "Our little village doesn't usually have much need for these. As far as I know, Ezra is the only one who has one, and it is part of a sacred healing tool she brought back with her from her travels many years ago. This one, though, will go a long way towards restocking the village. Thank you, Kryda." Marcus pocketed the pearl and smiled gratefully at the dwarf. Her simple gift would help provide for his village for months to come.

* * *

Kryda almost wanted to stay when she saw the amount of food the villagers had packed for her. They had been so generous that she was forced to leave behind some of the heavier, fresher items in favor of dry, bland foods that would last through her trip. There was simply too much for her to take.

"I won't be needin' to hunt any time soon, tha's for sure." Kryda laughed as Marcus handed her another carefully wrapped portion of dried game. "Hell, I probably won't even need to eat again for another three days!" She patted her belly, still full from the feast, and Marcus smiled back at her.

"We had been preparing for the beast to keep us holed up in our village for some time…so we held a lot of food in reserve. Now that we can gather freely from the land again, we won't need all of these preserves. And you're the reason for that, so the village wants you to have as much of it as you need."

"It's amazin' that you've still got so much."

"We all sold many of our belongings to the merchants to be sure we had enough food. We'll be able to replace all of that once I sell your pearl, though." Marcus fingered the gem through his pocket, still shocked that something so small could be so valuable.

"Well, I'm all ready to go." Kryda patted her full-to-bursting pack, then grimaced at Marcus. "Feels like it'll be slow going the first couple of days, but it'll be worth it in the end to be well fed," she quipped.

Marcus reached out to shake Kryda's hand, but she pulled him into a tight hug, which he returned gratefully. She pulled away after a few long moments

CHAPTER 4

and hefted her pack onto her back with considerable effort. It was nearly as big as she.

"Thank you again, Kryda," Marcus said quietly, clasping her free hand in his. "For everything."

* * *

As Kryda stepped out into the late morning sunshine, she spotted the little girl, flouncing through the village square and humming to herself. Kryda called her over, and the little girl immediately ran to her and flung herself into Kryda's arms, nearly bowling her over.

"What's yer name, little lass?" Kryda asked.

"Lucinia," the little girl replied, looking up at Kryda with huge, joyful eyes.

"Well, little Lucy, I have something for you." Kryda knelt down, pulling a fine cord from her belt pouch that had a small pearl strung onto it. "This is a *very* special pearl," Kryda told her, holding out the necklace. "I donae want ye to be sellin' it, no matter what a merchant offers ye for it, ye hear?"

"Oh, it's beautiful!" Lucinia exclaimed as Kryda tied the necklace around her neck, then rocked back on her heels to look at her. The girl touched it reverently, lifting it in front of her face to admire it. "It makes me want to sing!"

"You sing yer little heart out, Lucy me lass," Kryda said thickly, swallowing a lump in her throat. "Ye heard the old crone last night; that's the medicine yer people be needin' right now." She patted the girl's head one last time, then stood back up and looked around the village. Most of the village was busy cleaning up the remains of the feast or preparing to venture out into the newly healed land for some much needed gathering, hunting, and freedom.

Kryda started toward the gate, hoping to avoid a fuss over her departure. She was grateful that the villagers seemed to notice her eagerness to leave, and simply paused in their tasks to wave and shout their goodbyes as she passed. Marcus and his mother emerged from their home to walk silently behind her, joined by Ezra the healer and little Lucy. When they reached the northern gates, Kryda turned to say her final farewell, but the words caught in her throat. She nodded to her newfound friends, then stepped through the gates and into the next stage of her adventure.

5

Chapter 5

The Lower City

It was already later in the day than Kryda would have liked, and with the weight of her pack bearing down on her with every step, she knew she'd have to make camp earlier than she normally would. She would also have to take the time to tie her pack out of reach of scavengers to protect her food for the night Luckily, at least the weather looked to be in her favour.

She pressed on through the heat of the day, a damp scrap of cloth tied around her forehead to keep her cool, and drank only sparingly of her ale, downing mostly water instead. Kryda wanted to ensure that she didn't run out of the refreshing ale before she reached the city.

In terms of food, the rich farewell feast the villagers had fed her continued to sustain her for most of the day, so she didn't need to stop to eat. By the time the light was beginning to fade, she felt she'd actually made very good time. Deciding that she wouldn't need a fire or a shelter on such a beautiful night, Kryda took the opportunity to simply rest against the grassy earth and watch the sunset through the trees.

Just before the last rays of sunlight dissolved, Kryda tied her pack high up in the trees, then climbed down to lay out her bedroll. She stretched out with a sigh, staring up at the sky as she waited for the stars to come out. She had just glimpsed a single winking pinpoint of light before she drifted off into a deep, dreamless sleep.

She awoke to a rustling in the nearby bushes, and reached slowly for the knife in her pack. Two rambunctious squirrels burst from the foliage, chasing other around the trees. They wove here and there before scampering directly across Kryda's legs, which were still covered by her blanket. She grinned and lay back, content to allow the little creatures to play. There was no need for her to hunt; she hardly even had any room for more food in her pack in the first place.

She climbed the tree to retrieve her pack, preparing herself some fresh fruit and ale for breakfast in the faint light of the false dawn. She was grateful that she could save time on hunting thanks to her full pack, but as long as the weather held up, she'd also be able to forego making and breaking camp. Eager to resume her journey, she quickly fastened her bedroll to her pack and continued north.

The day was a bit cooler than the previous one had been, and Kryda found a stream around midday. She paused to rest, eat, and refill her water canteen. While dipping it in the fresh stream, she spotted some mushrooms, and decided that they'd pair quite well with some ale for lunch.

When she departed from the stream, she felt greatly renewed in spirit, and the rest of the day progressed with little excitement and no mishaps. As evening approached, Kryda began to notice the weather changing, and decided to find a place to set up camp. Eventually, she came upon a small cave. After gathering some kindling, she ducked into the cave and soon had a small, bright fire burning. It didn't give off much in the way of heat, but by the time Kryda finished adding her last log to the little bonfire, she was sweating profusely.

She sat beside the fire, breathing heavily. Her heart was pounding in her chest, each beat rattling her ribcage. Staring into the flames, she saw her

CHAPTER 5

village—her family, Lan, all with animals following closely at their heels, but none of them seemed to notice. An owl perched on her mother's shoulder, and a bear lumbered along behind her father. Mice scurried around Fáelán's feet. She saw herself, a little girl again, talking to a fluffy wolf pup as it sat in front of her, its little head tilted, ears flopping to the side.

Then the vision changed, and she saw the wolf from her earlier visions. It was facing down the corrupted boar in the forest, growling, its hackles raised. She watched with bated breath, but a sound behind her turned her head, and she saw Marcus approaching her. He emerged from the bushes, crouched, staring at her with his hand extended.

"Easy, there," he murmured, his eyes wide. Kryda realized with a shock that his eyes were green with slitted pupils, like a cat's. He reached out cautiously to lay a hand on her head. She tried to speak, but the words tangled in an unfamiliar tongue and teeth, and the only sound that emerged was a low whine.

The vision changed again. She was staring down at the pitiful corpse of the yearling boar. She heard a whine behind her, and whirled around to see Marcus, his hand resting on the head of a massive wolf. He looked up at her curiously.

"How did you manage to tame this wolf?" he asked.

"I dunae what yer talkin' about," she muttered. "He's not mine."

The wolf crouched low and growled at her, and Marcus stepped back, his catlike gaze flicking between her and the snarling wolf.

"Go on back where ye came from, ye overgrown mutt!" she shouted. The wolf leaped at her.

* * *

Kryda gasped for air, sweat trickling down her forehead. She had fallen asleep dangerously close to the fire, but she suspected it had less to with the fire than with her strange dreams. She shivered, rubbing her aching shoulder.

Her hand came away bloody. Eyes widening, she tugged her shirt to the side and saw three short gouges torn into her shoulder like claw marks.

"Ugh, I musta had a bit too much o' the ale last night," she grumbled. "What did I fall on to?" She ran her hand over the ground, searching for sharp rocks, but found nothing that could have left her with these cuts. Shaking her head, she pulled off her shirt and dabbed at the wound, tearing a strip from the bottom to bandage it. She'd wash it when she came to the next stream.

Exhaustion fogged her vision and she sank back to the floor. When she awoke again, her head was pounding, just like it had after the first night she'd been allowed to drink as much ale as she wanted. *I didnae have enough ale to feel this terrible*, she thought, picking up her wineskin. It was still half full. "There's somethin' not right..." she mused.

Stumbling out of the cave, she looked up at the sun in the east, then stared north, wondering how far she still had to go before she'd reach the city. Glancing to the west, she decided the road was closer than the mountain pass, even if it was riskier.

Gathering her belongings, Kryda nibbled on a crust of bread as she headed east toward the road, but it didn't settle well in her stomach. She reached for her canteen and sloppily gulped down the water, carelessly allowing it to spill out of the corners of her mouth. When she finally reached the side of the road, she dropped her pack, then sat and leaned on it, waiting for a cart to pass by.

***

Traz whistled cheerfully to himself, lightly drawing the reins along his ponies' backs as he drove his cart toward the city. A huddled lump on the side of the road caught his eye, and he clucked his tongue, commanding the ponies to stop. Hopping down from his cart, he went over to check on the creature. It was a dwarf, curled up and sleeping like a stone. Traz was shocked that the noise he'd been making wasn't enough to wake her. Was she even still alive?

CHAPTER 5

He nudged one of her legs with his foot to try and rouse her, but she did not stir. He scanned her belongings, and the gleam of a dwarven pickaxe caught his eye. He squinted, trying to make out the name carved into the handle.

"Fáelán? Seems a strange name for a woman, even for the dwarves," he muttered to himself. *Poor thing...*he thought. "Ah, well," he sighed. "At least that fine piece of craftsmanship won't go to waste." He reached for the pickaxe, but his skinny arm was immediately imprisoned in an iron grip, stocky fingers closing around his wrist.

"What're ya doin' touchin' me pick?" Kryda demanded, her voice thick and groggy.

"Oh, forgive me, ma'am, I was...uh...just checking the name here, as it seemed you may have been in need of some assistance," he babbled. Kryda released his arm and he straightened, brushing his overcoat back into place. "My name is Traz, and I am on my way to Starting City." He cleared his throat and bowed deeply with a flourish.

"As am I." Kryda stood up, brushing the dirt from her trousers. Although she was only a few inches taller than the kender, her bulk made her seem much bigger. "I also be carryin' far too much food for just me. Take me with ye, and ye can have this bag o' fresh food for yer troubles." She passed the kender her bag, which was nearly half as big as he was. Traz opened it and peeked inside as Kryda tossed her pack into the back of the wagon.

This is real quality produce! he thought to himself. *This'll pay my way for at least a couple of days at that crummy inn. Their food is terrible. I know the cook will be glad to have something fresh to work with from the country!* Traz was so enamored with his good luck that he almost forgot to bargain with the dwarf.

"Not so fast there—" He eyed the pickaxe again, trying to recall her name. "Faye! These victuals are nearly spoiled, and I won't be able to eat them all before they do!" He gestured at his scrawny frame with an apologetic bow.

"Faye?" Kryda's eyes followed his. "Oh, tha'...." She shook her head. "Name's Kryda. Traz, are ye tellin' me that ye know not a soul in tha' city who would treat ye like a king fer that? It's from the village to the south and they have the best farmland this side of the mountains. Well, if ye'd rather coin..."

The kender's eyes sparkled as Kryda reached into her pouch, but he fought back a scowl when her hand emerged with only two silver coins in her palm. Kryda knew the food was worth much more.

"I suppose I could find someone," Traz conceded grudgingly. "We wouldn't want it to go to waste, now would we?" Kryda shrugged, her expression blank, and dropped the coins back into her pouch. "So what brings you to the wondrous Starting City?" he ventured, his curiosity getting the better of him.

"I'll just be passin' through. May find me some work...doin' somtin' er other."

"I could possibly help you with that....for a fee, of course," he offered, rubbing his hands together thoughtfully. "What are you good at?"

"Swingin' this pick has been my life so far, but I dunae if it's gonna be of any help up here...I be good with me fists too, though. Certain that'll come in handy in a city." The kender opened his mouth to reply, but Kryda cut him off. "I can find me own way, though. Thanks fer the offer, but I'm travelin' on a budget, ya know."

Traz closed his mouth and shrugged nonchalantly. "Understandable, of course. I will give you this piece of advice for free, though: you should introduce yourself at the Academy of the Adventurer's Guild. In case you find yourself in need of some other connections, I'll be staying at the Crowe's Nest." Traz smiled broadly and bowed once again, gesturing for Kryda to climb atop his cart.

* * *

There was very little chat as the two completed the trek to the city, and it was nearly dusk before they parted ways at the Crowe's Nest. Kryda had expected Traz's inn of choice to be full of kenders, and it turned out to be just

CHAPTER 5

so. She briefly inspected her pack to ensure that everything was still there and waved politely to Traz as she left, more to keep her eyes on him for as long as possible than out of real courtesy. She had noticed he was clutching the bag of food tightly and eyeing the other kenders. He had been pleasant enough, but she had decided to keep her distance. She still didn't trust his intentions.

Once she felt she was at a safe distance from the kenders, she took a moment to appreciate the city. She'd seen a few cities while on delivery trips with her father, but she'd always stayed in camp to admire their beauty from afar while he took the goods into the city. From within, Starting City was overwhelmingly exciting. There were people bustling about everywhere, calling out their wares or entertaining passerby with song, dance and acrobatics. Most were clearly aiming to turn a profit, but at this time of night, some were out simply because they'd had more than their share of wine or ale.

She paused to take stock of her supplies. Her wineskin could do with a refill, and although she still had plenty of food even after surrendering her bag to Traz, she thought it might be nice to have some freshly prepared meat. Surely a respectable inn wouldn't balk at the opportunity to trade for some fresh vegetables. But she wasn't yet ready to settle in for the night; she wanted to explore this wondrous place.

The kender had told her to head toward the inner city to find the Adventurer's Guild. She made her way through the winding streets, passing all manner of shops. A weaver was selling all manner of stout fabrics, as well as various luxury textiles from across the continent. Just beyond the weaver, an armorer was peddling leather that looked more suitable for shoes than combat, but he was trying to convince anyone who would listen that there were adventures to be had, and that he was the one to equip them. As Kryda passed him, she eyed a pair of bracers that were noticeably higher quality than the rest of his wares. The vendor took note of her interest, and shifted his attention to her.

"You'll not find a better deal for that kind of craftsmanship, let me tell you!" he called. Intrigued, Kryda made her way over to him, and he nodded to the bracers. They were short and thick, probably intended for the forearms of a heavy blacksmith. "Try them on," the vendor offered. Kryda slipped them onto her forearms; they fit almost perfectly. They were soft and breathable on the inside, but hard as bone on the outside. Despite herself, Kryda was impressed.

"Did'ye make these yerself?" she inquired, tapping her fingers on the solid leather.

"My daughter did, actually. Only ten years old and already surpassing her dear old father," he beamed. "Mind you, she does get the best materials I can find her. I spare no expense for such a talent." He glanced toward the back of his cart, and to her surprise, Kryda saw the little girl sleeping soundly upon a pile of furs. "She wanted to come with me today so very badly, to see the sale of her work." He glanced hopefully at Kryda, but was disappointed to see her already removing the bracers. But Kryda wasn't finished yet.

"Of course she would...and I have some very special things for her, if ye'd be so kind as to hold on to these for me 'til the morn.'"

"But of course!" the vendor cried, his face lighting up again. "I was about to close up shop for the night anyway—oh! She'll be so thrilled!" He checked himself, hoping his pride in his daughter's craftsmanship hadn't allowed him to get too carried away. "About the price, though...it is a *very* fine piece of work..." He looked Kryda over, wondering what she had to offer. She didn't look to him like a warrior or a merchant, but had clearly been travelling for some time, and dwarves weren't a common sight in this city. *She must be delivering some goods*, he decided.

Kryda reached into her pouch and pulled out one of the pearls. The vendor's eyes widened, and he opened his mouth to speak, but Kryda held a finger to her lips as she closed her hand around the gem again. "Let it be a surprise for the lass. It's more special than ye know. I wouldnae sell one o' these ones to the merchant who comes 'round me village—wouldna even tell 'em about it."

"Then why...?"

"She do have a talent, tha' one. She'll be seein' me again." Dipping her head in farewell, Kryda continued on through the lower market, enjoying the

CHAPTER 5

bustle of the city. She made only one more stop before leaving the merchant square—to acquire some blow darts.

6

Chapter 6

The Adventurers

Kryda found an inn to settle into for the night, just outside the perimeter of the upper terrace that housed the Academy of the Adventurer's Guild. She hopped onto a barstool and ordered a pint of the house brew. After a sip and a nod to the barkeep, she turned on her stool to survey the other patrons. There were some obvious regulars, some guttersnipes—likely hoping to brush shoulders with the city dwellers and local merchants, fishing for jobs and a way out of the alleys—plenty of traveling merchants enjoying some rare camaraderie, and a particularly rowdy group of patrons sporting crude armour and weapons.

They must be adventurers, Kryda thought, and decided to go introduce herself. One of the adventurers, a human woman, seemed to be having a friendly argument with a gnome about how best to woo a woman. Spotting Kryda's approach, the woman called to her.

"Hey, you with the pickaxe! Come over here and help me educate this bastard—he seems to think that the best way to get a girl's attention is to weep all over her."

"I never said I would 'weep all over her'! I simply said that women appreciate someone who isn't afraid to show emotion!" protested the gnome.

"But your idea of 'showing emotion' is to snot on her shoulder while telling her the tragic tale of your sad, lonely life!"

The table erupted in such a cacophony of shouts and howls of laughter that Kryda couldn't make out a single word of the gnome's reply.

"Depends on tha woman," she cut in with a shrug. The table fell silent for a moment as the group appraised her. After a moment, the woman rolled her eyes playfully, as if her game had been spoiled, before bursting into laughter again.

"Of course it does!" she exclaimed, "but that wouldn't make for very good banter, now would it? What would seal the deal for *you*, sweetheart?" Without missing a beat, Kryda simply raised her glass, earning an uproar of hoots, hollers and clinks. "Another round for our new friend!" the woman cried, beckoning to Kryda. "I'm Leeta. That there lover boy is Fankin, and over there are Paddy, Kurt, and Odo. Come, sit and drink with us!"

"Thank ye! Name's Kryda. Do ye be part of the Adventurer's Guild?"

"Yes, but we're still in training. It's tough, but pays well, even for us trainees. I can't wait to get out there on some real contracts, though." She placed one hand on the hilt of her sword. Fankin rolled his eyes and brought the conversation back to romance.

"What do you think it'd take for *that* one?" He asked, jerking his chin toward the barmaid as she walked away, his beady eyes clearly following her petite elven behind as she wiggled her way through the crowd.

"*Tha'* one wants tae see yer *emotions!*" Kryda jeered, prodding Fankin's arm teasingly.

"No way! A girl can't be soft like that and work in a place like this!" he protested.

"Tha's exactly why! She deals wi' all these drunks all night; she wants tae go home ta someone quiet and affectionate."

"Haven't you ever seen a drunk get all emotional? Like that old bastard over there." Fankin pointed to an old man who looked like he hadn't left that spot in three days. "He's here all the time. You just watch. One or two more drinks and he's going to start wandering all over with his sad story, wailing to anyone too kind to tell him to sod off. Nah, that girl wants none of that when she gets home. She wants someone strong and stable."

"I bet ye a pint tha' ye canae take her to yer room without gettin' *emotional*."

"You're on!" Fankin slammed his ale down on the table, splashing Leeta, who was laughing too hard to care.

"There's not a single stoic bone in your body, Fankin," she teased him.

"Do you want to come watch, just to be sure??" he demanded.

"Nah, you're a terrible liar. I'll know when you come back."

"You'll know when I *don't* come back!" he declared, downing the last of his ale and wandering off to woo the barmaid. Kryda and Leeta were now laughing so hysterically that they were hard pressed to drink the toast they'd raised to him for good luck. When they finally managed to compose themselves, they returned to their conversation about the guild.

"So you have an interest in the guild, do you?" Leeta prodded.

"Aye. I do be stayin' the night here, but will be gettin' up to the guild in the morn."

Leeta seemed delighted that Kryda would be joining the guild, and was saying something about hoping they'd be placed in the same squad, but Kryda was distracted by a man who had just walked in. His blond hair was cropped short, and he was dressed nicely enough that he stood out as a man who was clearly not from this part of the city. He seemed to be looking for someone. The barmaid rushed to greet him, and the man flashed her a vibrant smile, leaning down to whisper something that made her laugh.

Kryda paid little mind as Fankin stormed back to the table and slouched back into his chair, grumbling that he would have had a full night, if *he* hadn't come in just then. As Kryda watched, the barmaid pointed directly at the table where she was sitting. Kryda looked away quickly, hoping the man hadn't noticed her staring.

Leeta got to her feet and called to the blond man. "Harden! Over here!" She sat back down, waiting for him to make his way over to their table. "I

CHAPTER 6

was wondering when you'd show up to 'collect' us," she grinned. The blond man took a seat across from Kryda and nodded towards her.

"Who's this?" he asked. Leeta looked mildly surprised that he'd brushed off her friendly greeting.

"Right. Harden, sir, meet Kryda. Kryda, this is our head trainer, Captain Harden." Leeta slouched back down in her chair and reached for her mug of ale. "She's joining up tomorrow."

"Really?" Harden half-stood to extend his arm across the table toward Kryda, who had to stand up fully to reach his hand. His grip was surprisingly strong for a human. "It's not very often we see dwarves around. I'm sure you'll make a wonderful addition to our team. What's your specialty?"

The barmaid set out another round on the table as Kryda sat back down, Harden's warm welcome putting her at ease. "I've always been a miner, but I've recently discovered that me pick can be used for many a thing." She smiled fondly at the memory, then hastily added, "Sir." He waved a hand dismissively and smiled back at her.

"No need for the formality here, and you're obviously not accustomed to it. No other combat training as of yet, then?"

"No, sir, only hunting."

He nodded. "You'll be with me, then." Leeta and the other adventurers raised their glasses to that with shouts of approval, and Harden chuckled. "Seems you've made friends with the crew already. You won't be with them for a few days yet, though. I have a meeting tomorrow, so you'll have plenty of time to rest after your travels. Orientation will be in two days. I'll expect you to report to the gates of the Academy at sunrise; I'll meet you there to help you get settled, and I'll have Connahay handle the others' training."

"Great," Leeta muttered, taking another swig of her ale. Kryda grinned. She had no idea who Connahay was, but she had a feeling she was going to enjoy her time at the Academy.

Harden polished off his own mug of ale with impressive speed before speaking again. "Come on, you lot, let's get back before the other officers find out that I come here to do more than just round up my unruly squadron of adventurers." The rest of the group finished off their own ales and stood with a chorus of farewells. Kryda lifted her glass to them as they left, and quickly downed the rest of her ale.

When the barmaid came back around, Kryda decided to order a stew and a hot cider to combat the evening chill. While she was waiting for her meal to arrive, she noticed that the old man Fankin pointed out earlier had indeed begun to wander the tavern in search of a sympathetic ear. As the barmaid emerged from the kitchen with Kryda's stew, he collided with her, nearly knocking it from her arms. It sloshed around, spilling over her arms. She winced, but kept her grip, growling in frustration.

"Gibbs, please go sit down somewhere. You know I don't like it when I have to turn you out."

"I'm sorry, Eilly! Is your hand alright? Let me see—"

She twisted away from him. "I'm *fine*, Gibbs, just go find a seat." Gibbs shuffled away dejectedly, and the girl set the stew down on the bar and went to clean off her hand.

Kryda watched as the old man headed back toward his little corner of solitude, casting concerned glances over his shoulder toward the young woman he'd injured with his carelessness. He looked so lost and unhappy that Kryda felt the need to reach out to him.

"Hey, old man Gibbs! Come on over and sit here with me."

He brightened immediately and trotted over to her table. He peered at her, looking a bit confused. "Have we met?" he asked.

"Nah, I overheard yer name. I'm Kryda. Pleased to meet you."

"A pleasure." He bowed gracefully, which surprised Kryda—not only because he didn't particularly look like a gentleman, but also because she was shocked the inebriated old man hadn't completely lost his balance. He plopped down in the chair next to Kryda, just as the barmaid approached with Kryda's stew.

"Another ale for me, please, Eilly," he mumbled.

"No, Gibbs," she said flatly, setting down Kryda's stew and cider. "Is he bothering you?" she asked Kryda, pursing her lips and setting her hands on her hips, which were much more ample than Kryda would have expected of an elf. No wonder Fankin had taken such an interest in her.

CHAPTER 6

"He's harmless, I'm sure. I invited him over."

To Kryda's surprise, the woman looked relieved, possibly even gratified, at her reply. *Aye, emotional*, Kryda thought, smiling to herself. "Well, alright then. If you need anything, just wave me over." Kryda and Gibbs sat silently, watching the barmaid go, until she stopped looking back at them and disappeared into the kitchen.

Gibbs was the first to speak. "I saw you sitting here with the adventurers. Are you in the Guild as well? I've never seen you around here before."

"I just got to the city today, and I'll be meeting with the Guild in a few days to get signed up."

"Wonderful!" Gibbs exclaimed. "I was an adventurer myself in my youth, you know. Back in my day—" Gibbs launched into a full account of his training and adventures, his life of luxury and love, as well as stories of where things had gone wrong in his life. He was a very good storyteller, and Kryda enjoyed listening to him as she ate her stew and sipped her cider.

As Gibbs got further into his life story, however, his words became more and more slurred, and his voice more broken. Kryda learned that he'd lost his wife and son a few years back—that must have been what led him to this life, sitting in the same bar night after night, just searching for some companionship—but the old man was becoming nearly incomprehensible by this point. Kryda tried to calm him down, but her attempts only seemed to make him more upset. The barmaid saw him weeping inconsolably and came rushing over.

"There, there, Gibbs, come along. Let's get you on home now."

When he heard her voice, he turned to her and grasped at her arms, looking up at her pleadingly.

"Oh, please, Eilatra, I'm just telling a story to my new friend here. I promise—"

Eilatra cut him off. "You and I both know what it means when you get to this story, Gibbs," she said quietly. The old man bowed his head, but complied, stumbling up from his chair. Eilatra caught him, but his weight and uncontrolled momentum nearly knocked her over. Kryda leaped up to help, pulling his other arm over her shoulders. Working together, they steered the old man toward the front door, but Kryda didn't want the old man to be left in the chill night air.

"How far is his house? I'll take him," she offered.

"Oh, you don't need to do that," the barmaid protested, and Kryda once again glimpsed a look of pleasant surprise and gratitude. "He makes his way home eventually." But she, too, did not look pleased with the prospect of making him stumble home on his own.

"It'd be no trouble at all, really," Kryda insisted.

"Well, if you're sure…it isn't very far, but I do worry. It's six houses down on the left; the one with the red door. I'm always telling him to leave a light burning outside before he comes. I hope he remembered this time."

Kryda nodded, shifting more of the man's weight onto herself and easing him off of Eilatra. As Kryda headed out the door with Gibbs in tow, the barmaid called after her, her beautiful elven voice ringing with sincerity.

"Thank you!"

CHAPTER 6

7

Chapter 7

The Bargain

Kryda strolled slowly back to the tavern, reminiscing on her own heartache over the life she'd left behind. The tavern was quieter now, but her wineskin, which she'd filled in preparation for tomorrow, was now empty. She made a beeline straight for the bar, and asked Eilatra for a shot. The barmaid poured two—one for herself, and one for the dwarf—so she could raise a toast to Kryda for her kindness to the old man. They downed the burning liquor, then sat in silence for a few moments.

"I knew his son," Eilatra began, rolling the shot glass between her fingers, "before he went missing. He was a charming young man, and we were becoming friends. It could have been more, had we been given the time. He took good care of his father after his mother died, and when he didn't come home, Gibbs became obsessed with finding him. Someone had to take care of the old man. At first, I just brought him a decent meal every so often, and tried to make sure he was still eating well. But he got worse, and soon I was spending more and more time tidying his house and trying to talk the old man out of his obsession. He wouldn't have left the house at all, if I hadn't insisted on a walk every now and then. Sometimes, just to get him out and about, I'd tell him that I needed his help with something. And then one day, he just wandered in here all on his own, and sat right in that corner." She gestured to where Gibbs had been slumped over earlier.

"He was visibly exhausted—both physically and emotionally—but you could see that his mind was still going. It wouldn't let him rest. He's been here almost every day since, and that was several months ago. I always make sure he eats something, and he'll have a few drinks, just to get his mind to slow down so he can sleep. However, as you saw tonight, he often loses control, and it all comes crashing down on him again. At least his heavy drinking still makes him sleep. As a matter of fact, he probably won't even be well enough to come back tomorrow night," she sighed, tapping her fingers against her glass and staring off into the distance, clearly embroiled in her own thoughts.

"I'll take him some dinner, of course," she sniffled, smiling sadly at Kryda as the tears brimmed in her eyes. "Thank you again for helping him tonight. It means a lot to me." Kryda nodded solemnly, tapping her glass to Eilatra's. She sat in silence for a moment, studying the elf, before sighing heavily.

"S'pose it wouldn't hurt either of us to 'ave another."

* * *

Eilatra cleared out the last of the tavern's drunken patrons, either kicking them out or sending them to their rooms, and cleaned off the bar. When she'd finished closing up, she woke Kryda, who had slumped over the bar in a drunken stupor. She led Kryda upstairs to help her get settled in her room, and on the way up the stairs, Kryda began to spill all of her troubles onto the elf woman's shoulder, telling her all about the life she'd left behind, the life she could've had with Lan.

When they reached her room, Eilatra helped Kryda remove her armour and outer garments, trying to make out the rest of the story as Kryda trailed off, drifting back to sleep. "I donae e'en know wha' I'm out 'ere fer," were her last words before she collapsed, unconscious, across the bed. Her accent was thick and the words were slurred, but Eilatra knew that Kryda was feeling lost, wished there were something she could do to help ease the pain.

Eilatra sat on the edge of the bed for a few moments, watching Kryda sleep. She was grateful for the kindness the dwarf had shown to both her and Gibbs, even though she hadn't really needed the help. She wet a rag in the washbowl that beside the bed and gently washed Kryda's tear-streaked face, before pulling the blankets lightly over the sleeping dwarf. She hung up the armour, kindled a fire to take the chill out of the room, and gathered Kryda's clothes to be washed. Pausing on her way out the door, she took one last lingering look at the sleeping dwarf. "Thank you again," she murmured, smiling, and then snuffed the torch and quietly closed the door.

* * *

Morning came far too quickly, signalled by a narrow beam of light peeking through the dark curtains. Rolling over with a groan, Kryda reached for her wineskin, but found it empty. Rubbing her eyes, she let the empty container fall to the floor, and gazed thoughtfully around the room, and then at herself. She was in her smallclothes. *How did that happen?* she wondered, then briefly remembered the barmaid helping her get into bed. *What was her name again? Aiyla...Eyelot...ugh! My head is killing me!*

Rolling off the bed and struggling to her feet, Kryda found her clothes and a spare shift, clean and folded, on the bench at the end of the bed. Her boots were tucked neatly underneath the bed, and her armor, also cleaned, hung in the corner. A fresh washbowl had been set on the nightstand, still warm enough to fog up the bottom of the looking glass.

She started to wet the rag that had also been left for her, preparing to scrub the grime of travel off her face, but when she looked in the glass, she saw that her face was already clean. Splashing some water on herself anyway, she tried to recall the previous night. Staring into the bowl of rippling water, each small wave seemed to hold a fraction of a memory. Had she really cried? Had she really told her story to this complete stranger? No one was supposed to see her weaknesses—the only one who ever had was Lan, who had watched her as she nearly drowned.

* * *

Kryda wanted more than anything to go back to sleep, but briefly recalled the little armourer's daughter from the market, and knew she had a bargain to strike. She didn't stop for food or drink on her way out of the tavern, knowing she'd get both from the market on her way back. Heading out of the city the same way she'd come in, she made the trip much more quickly than she had the night before. For one thing, she was on a mission now, and for another, she also wasn't carrying her hefty pack.

The merchants were just beginning to wake and set up shop, so she wasn't tempted to stop and look. Even the guards at the south gate were not quite awake yet, and didn't pay much mind to her as she exited the city. She had come in on the road with the kender, but that she hadn't been noting the lay of the forest as they travelled. She knew just where to go to find what she was looking for.

Creeping quietly through the bushes, she travelled at an angle away from both the city and the roadway. As soon as they were both out of sight and the bustling noise of city life began to fade, she began her search for tracks. Pausing to pick some ripe berries from a bush, Kryda spotted a set of long, thin prints nearby. She was in luck; the rabbit tracks were still fresh. Following them deeper into the forest, she paused as she laid eyes on the most beautiful white rabbit she'd ever seen. This was much more than she'd hoped for.

Drawing the blow darts and tube from her belt pouch, she dipped the darts in a small solution meant to stun small game. Taking a deep breath, she aimed for the fatty rump of the animal, which was poking up proudly from the bush where it was munching on some clover. With one swift puff of air through the tube, the dart zipped into the bush, directly to the left of the rabbit. It leaped up with a start, hopping away from the bush, its small nose flaring as it searched for the source of the disturbance.

Kryda cursed quietly, lowering her body closer to the ground behind a shrub. There were twigs scattered all across the ground, and with the bunny on high alert, she didn't dare to allow her body to touch the ground. Holding herself just above the ground, her arms trembling with the strain, she listened carefully for the rabbit.

Her left hand began to ache from the pressure of the tube between her fingers and her head pounded from both her hangover and the lack of oxygen from her shallow breathing. Sweat beaded on her forehead, and the grass beneath her fingers grew slippery with sweat. Finally, after what seemed like an eternity, she heard the rabbit shift.

It was only when she finally heard the faint sound of contented munching that she dared shift her weight again and take a deep breath. Moving as silently as she could, she straightened her arms, bottom in the air, and carefully moved her hands nearer her feet, away from the twigs that had been beneath her belly.

Bending her knees into a crouch, she lifted her arms from the ground and stretched her fingers and shoulders. She pivoted slowly, then stepped to the other side of the shrub. She could just barely make out the white rabbit's tail, now slightly further into the forest.

Searching for another hiding place closer to the new bush where the rabbit had taken up breakfast, Kryda suddenly remembered Marcus and his trees. Kryda was good at climbing trees, but she was more accustomed to climbing them for fun, not to hunt. She spotted the perfect tree—one branch hanging over a clearing near the bunny's bush.

The branch was beyond her reach, but there was a thin sapling sprouting up next to the larger one, which Kryda thought she might be able to climb

CHAPTER 7

hand over hand like a rope. She only hoped it would be strong enough to hold her weight. Rising from her crouch, she crept over to the little tree.

Carefully cupping her hands around the trunk of the tree, Kryda gripped it tightly and began to climb. She shuffled up slowly, pushing herself up with her feet. Pausing about halfway up, she glanced back at the rabbit, fully aware that its delicate ears were twitching anxiously towards every sound. Slowly straightening her legs, Kryda reached up higher. The young tree swayed with her movement, and the branch of the bigger tree was still slightly out of reach.

Concentrating hard on her task, Kryda was startled by a sound nearby, but it was only a squirrel jumping from one tree to another. The rabbit's ears twitched, but it was not bothered by the noise. This made Kryda more confident that her own movements in the trees wouldn't startle it again.

With another awkward shuffle upwards, Kryda ascended higher up the sapling, which was beginning to bend under her weight. She stretched out one arm toward the branch—she was high enough now to reach it, but still too far away. She eased her weight forward, and slowly but surely, the sapling began to bend towards the larger tree. Very carefully, Kryda slid her pickaxe out of her belt, gripping it near the end of the handle. Her wrists were sore, which made it difficult to hold the imbalanced weight of it, but she was able to hook one edge of it over the branch, pulling herself the extra few inches it took for her to get her hand around the branch. She gripped tightly to her perch with her legs, lest the sound of the sapling snapping back upright would startle the rabbit. Clutching the branch firmly with one hand, she let go of the pickaxe with the other, and gripped the branch tightly with both hands. She slowly let her legs slip away from the skinny little sapling until she could hold no longer, and let it ease back to its natural position.

Swinging her freed legs up to the branch, Kryda held herself there, upside-down, trying to catch her breath. Scrambling up onto the branch, she tucked her pickaxe back into her belt, then crept along the length of the branch as far as she dared. Readying another blow dart, she watched the rabbit carefully for any change in its awareness, but it continued chewing placidly. Taking a deep breath, Kryda blew swiftly into the tube. Just as she did so, the branch snapped loudly, and Kryda tumbled into the brush with a crash.

"Chreach!" Kryda cursed, "At least I landed on me rump an' not me pick." She patted her treasured pickaxe, grateful it hadn't been damaged. She looked exasperatedly to the sky. "Brimir, I was aimin' for the rabbit's rump, not me own." She stood up and rubbed her bottom, realizing suddenly that something had broken—the vial of toxin. She felt around for broken shards to ensure there were none embedded in her flesh, but the vial was only cracked, and the pieces remained safely in her belt pouch.

Sighing in relief, she removed the pouch, careful not to touch the liquid. She'd have to rinse it off in a river, where it would be diluted enough to be safe. *So much fer huntin' today*, she thought, glancing regretfully back at the broken branch. To her delight, lying on the ground just a few feet away, was the white rabbit, a blow dart sticking straight up out of its rump.

"HA! Apologies an' thanks, Brimir!" Leaping up, Kryda hollered her excitement, but winced in pain when the landing jarred her aching rump and aggravated the pounding in her head. Gathering up the rabbit, she headed toward the stream to clean both it and herself before taking it back into the city.

* * *

When Kryda re-entered the city gates, the market was even busier than it had been when she came in the night before. Everything looked different in the light of day, and she had a hard time finding the armourer again, but he saw her as she passed by and called out to her. The little girl was sitting behind her father, eating her breakfast.

"So glad you could make it back!" the armourer greeted Kryda, then turned to his daughter. "Little one, this woman would like to speak with you."

"With me?" replied a little voice, with its mouth still half full.

"Yes, lass, with you," Kryda replied, smiling at the armourer's little protege. "I was walkin' by here last ev'n and spied a set o' bracers I swore'd been made by a master gnome! The ol' man 'ere says it's you I should be askin' about 'em."

The little girl's eyes widened, and she hastily gulped down the last of her food, darting over to the table to search for her bracers. "Where are they, father? You said you'd put them out!"

The armourer grinned. "Relax, little one, they're here. I kept them for her because she wanted to make the deal with you personally." He reached under the table for the box he'd hidden the bracers in, then passed it to his daughter. The little girl opened the box and beamed proudly as she displayed them to her customer.

"That'll be eighty gold pieces," she stated, matter-of-factly. Her father's eyes looked as if they'd pop right out of his head. He'd been asking fifty for them. Kryda grinned at the budding saleswoman.

"Twenty," she countered.

The girl's brow furrowed. "Sixty."

"Thirty."

The girl was getting a bit annoyed now, but she held her ground. "Sixty," she said, more adamantly. "When you said they must have been made by a master gnome, I thought you knew what you were talking about, but clearly you don't see their value—" She cut herself off, looking somewhat crushed, when she saw Kryda's shoulders shaking with laughter.

"I'm just messin' with ye, lass. I will give you thirty gold—" The girl closed the box and turned away, but Kryda continued as if she hadn't. "And…this."

Kryda held out the rabbit fur she'd cleaned earlier, gleaming white, with not a drop of blood to stain it. The armourer placed a hand on his daughter's shoulder, encouraging her to turn back around. When she did, her wet eyes went so wide that she nearly resembled a gnomish statue. "You'll still need to have the skin tanned, but I'd like for you to make me somethin' with these items."

The girl gave Kryda a quizzical look as she took the bundle of fur, realizing that there was something wrapped inside it as well. She retrieved a little box from inside the fur, and the tears escaped her eyes when she opened it to see the giant pearl contained within. She looked up at Kryda, speechless.

"Do we have a deal?" The girl nodded so enthusiastically that she almost dropped the pearl. "Good. Do what ye will with 'em, in yer own time, an' call on me at the Adventurer's Guild when yer done."

"Yes, ma'am."

"No need tae call me 'ma'am'. Kryda's me name." With that, Kryda handed over the gold and headed back to the inn, with a parting wave to the young armourer who was so clearly destined for greatness.

Chapter 8

The Inn

When she made it back to the inn, Kryda headed straight for her room, intending to get cleaned up. But when she got there, the lack of sleep and the exorbitant amount of spirits she'd consumed the night before finally caught up to her, and she collapsed onto her bed, asleep the moment her head touched the pillow.

When she awoke once more, she had no idea how long she'd been asleep, but she felt even worse than before. She was starting to suspect that she'd still been drunk earlier and her hangover was just kicking in now. She began to reach for her wineskin before she remembered that she'd left it empty. She thought of going downstairs to refill it, but her whole body ached. *Ugh... daft of me to let me drinkin' get out o' control*, she thought, hoping she hadn't made too much of a fool of herself in front of...*what was her name?*

Why do I even care so much?

Kryda was jolted out of her thoughts when she heard her door creak open.

"Oh, good, you're awake. I've brought you some wine to ease your head; I'm told that the only hangover cure for a dwarf is more of what started it in the first place, so here you are." Eilatra held out the stein for Kryda, who got up slowly, swaying a bit as she did so, and accepted the wine gratefully.

Kryda stared at the elf for a moment, then downed the wine in one go and sat heavily back down on the bed. Eilatra smiled slightly.

"Feeling better yet?"

"Aye, I s'pose I am." Kryda paused, wondering if she should say something about her earlier behavior. "Ah, about whatever I said last night...I-"

"Don't worry your pretty head about it. We can talk about that later if you'd like—at least, I hope we'll get a chance to talk again—and there's no need to apologize. For now, I've drawn you a bath, and I'll have someone bring your breakfast in here for you as well. I'm sure your head will thank you for not being down in the tavern; it's getting quite rowdy down there already. Here's a robe for you—I'll take your clothes down to be washed and warm a towel."

Eilatra entered the room to gather Kryda's dirtied boots and clothing into a basket, then headed back out, pausing in the doorway. She turned to face Kryda again, a small smile tugging at the corners of her lips. "Oh, and my name's Eilatra, in case you've forgotten. I wouldn't blame you—it's quite a mouthful for some folk, and you had a rough night."

Kryda was left sitting in stunned silence as the door closed behind Eilatra's glowing smile.

* * *

Refreshed by a few hours of sleep, Kryda prepared to head down for a bath. Her hangover had eased, as had the heat flooding the tips of her ears whenever she recalled the barmaid cheekily reminding her of her name. She was surprised when Eilatra met her again at the entrance to the baths, leading her to a private room supplied with more wine and scented oils. *Nae gonna happen*, Kryda thought grimly. *Me, smellin' of fruits and flowers? Nae very*

CHAPTER 8

likely. There were also a variety of scrub brushes and combs, and a pouch of herbs that smelled quite pleasant—and much less strongly than the oils. When Kryda picked it up to smell it, Eilatra detailed the contents.

"It's rosemary and skullcap. If you like the smell, just sprinkle some into the bath, or you can burn a little in the shell over there. It'll be good for your head…and for your heart." Eilatra reached up to touch Kryda's chest, but Kryda stepped back.

"I really don't need all this fussin'," she protested gruffly. "I just need to get clean." Her tone came out a little harsher than she meant it to, and she could see that Eilatra was a little hurt. She softened her voice and passed the pouch of herbs back to Eilatra, nodding to the bath. "They do smell good, though."

Eilatra tried to keep her expression neutral, but it was no use. Kryda had clearly already noticed that her words had hurt. She just couldn't seem to hide her emotions around Kryda, or keep them in check. Emptying the contents of the pouch into the warm bath, she stirred them gently into the water with one hand, deep in thought.

Kryda wasn't feeling like herself at all here…why did she feel the need to be so…gentle? Maybe she really did need that bath. Shaking her head, she determined that from now on, she'd be back to her usual fun-loving, carefree self.

"So, tell me," she began. "The clean armour, clothes…was i' you who did all o' that?"

Eilatra slowed what she was doing, more colour in her face than could be explained away by the steam rising from the hot water. She tried to keep her voice indifferent. "Yes, that was me."

"Well, I didn't realize all tha' was included when I paid fer my room. I certainly didn't expect any of this to be, either!" Kryda gestured to the bath, glancing around at the luxuries surrounding her.

Eilatra cleared her throat. She stood and straightened her skirts, trying her best to look professional.

"It isn't exactly…included. You helped, so I wanted to make you feel welcome."

"And that ye did!" Kryda replied with a grin. She was relieved to be acting more like herself again, but that's exactly what it felt like: an act. Why was she so muddled today? She turned to hang her robe on a peg, Eilatra turned away respectfully as Kryda stepped into the bath and sank gratefully into the warm, fragrant water with a loud sigh.

"I'll have your breakfast brought in," Eilatra told her, turning to leave Kryda to her bath.

"What'd ye mean by 'helped,' exactly?" Kryda called after her mischievously. Eilatra smiled a little to herself and turned back.

"Oh, just that you did something nice for me. Like, say, save me from the drunken ramblings of an old man." She batted her eyes dramatically at Kryda, who laughed as only a dwarf can laugh. "He'll talk your ear off if you let him, but he's harmless. Thank you for helping him return home safely."

"Well, you've more than made up for that little favor. I really appreciate yer hard work, Eilly, an' I'm sorry for the trouble. I was a mess...as far as I can remember."

Eilatra just smiled, walking back over to the bath and bending down to touch the water. "Is it still warm enough for you?"

The way Eilatra looked at her as she asked the simple question sent Kryda reeling out of her bravado and back into that same strange, awkward need to be gentle. She fought it away.

"Ah...aye, it's fine. To be honest, I'm still getting used to sittin' in this much warm water. Anything more than a sponge bath back home is a dip in the lake, and I'm the only one that...well, an' Lan..." She trailed off uncomfortably and stared into the herbs swirling around the water. *Come on, Kryda! Get it together! What are you doing?*

Eilatra smiled sympathetically, laying a hand on Kryda's shoulder. Kryda was too busy cursing herself for showing what she saw as weakness to bother stopping her this time.

"Would you like me to bring some more wine as well?"

"Aye, alright. Pass me my pouch and I'll give ye the coin for the food an' drink."

"No, no. It's on me." Eilatra stood and headed back out the door.

"I'm gonna tell the boss you deserve a raise or bonus or somethin' after all

CHAPTER 8

yer hard work!" Kryda called after her.

"Oh, I'm not working today," she called back, disappearing around the corner. Kryda chuckled to herself and settled back into the tub with another sigh. The scent of the herbs really was relaxing, and the wine was taking effect quickly in the heat and on an empty stomach. She found she was actually quite tired after her emotional night and drifted in and out of sleep with thoughts of home.

* * *

Fáelán was screaming. "Kryda!! NO!! KRYDAAAA!!!!" He waited for her to come up and held a breath, hoping beyond hope that she could hold hers longer than he could. When he finally had to gasp for air, she still hadn't come back up. He glanced around desperately for any way to get to her, but going around to the shore would take too long. Kryda was drowning and he was running out of time. He stood up, took a deep breath, and jumped.

Fáelán had no problem getting to Kryda; he sunk like a rock, but getting her out would not be easy. Grabbing hold of her with one arm and flailing the other to no avail, he decided to use what he knew: his legs and the ground. He walked awkwardly along the bottom of the lake, but his feet sank into the soft mud, and he was running out of breath. He was still far from the shallows, and the ground gave way under his feet over and over again. He caught a glimpse of a rock buried in the sludge, and made his way toward it. Glancing up at the surface, bubbles of air escaping from his lips as his lungs screamed for air, he could think of only one thing to do. He braced himself against the rock and jumped.

The force of his leap propelled the two of them upwards, and they breached the surface, gasping and choking. Fáelán struggled to keep them both afloat; Kryda weighed heavily on one arm, and he didn't even know what to do with the other. He'd seen some humans swimming once; it had looked so easy when they did it. Maybe their thinner bones were better suited to floating.

Trying to keep Kryda's head out of the water, he kicked furiously to keep himself at the surface, but his feet collided with Kryda's limp body. Her legs floated to the surface, and Fáelán realized that she suddenly felt much lighter. He leaned back, allowing his own legs to drift upwards as well, and found that it was much easier to stay up that way. For a moment, he just floated, trying to catch his breath, then carefully began to move his free arm and legs. After learning which way each movement would take him, it wasn't long before he managed to pull Kryda to shore.

"Now what?" he asked himself, and any gods that might be listening. Kryda looked deathly pale, but he refused to believe that she was dead. She wasn't breathing. The only thing Fáelán could think to do was to breathe for her. He tried to blow some air into her mouth, but it just came out of her nose. Refusing to give up, he plugged her nose with one hand and tried again. Her chest rose, but it did not fall. Frustrated and desperate, he pushed down hard on her chest, begging her to breathe.

The air wheezed out of her lungs as he pressed on her chest, her body twitching. This gave Fáelán hope that she might still be with him after all. He tried again, breathing into her mouth and pushing it back out, and each time her muscles seemed to react a little more strongly. Finally she gasped, her body curling up as she rolled to the side, and everything gushed out of her body at once: the water from her lungs and seemingly everything she'd eaten for the past week from her stomach. The vomiting lasted so long, Fáelán thought she might die from the exertion, but there was nothing he could do to stop it.

When it was finally over, she fell back and lay so still that he couldn't even bring himself to touch her. He held his breath, staring at the pale body in front of him, waiting for some sign of life. Finally, after what seemed a dangerously long time, her chest rose, held there for a moment, then fell. Her breaths were wheezing and uneven, but she was breathing.

Fáelán released the breath he'd been holding and fell back, exhausted, tears flooding his eyes as the terror subsided. It was getting late and the temperature was falling, and Fáelán knew Kryda would freeze to death if he didn't do something. He built a fire and stripped her of her wet clothing,

CHAPTER 8

hanging it to dry on nearby tree branches. He went back to the cliff to retrieve the cloak he'd shed, then brought it back and carefully covered Kryda's sleeping form.

It was night before she awoke. The moment he saw her stir, Fáelán bolted to her side. She blinked at him, then looked around, scowling and pulling the cloak more tightly around herself when she noticed her clothes drying in the trees.

Fáelán blushed furiously. "I'm sorry! I had to get your clothes…I mean, I didn't want you to catch cold and…well…I didn't know what else to do…"

Kryda cut him off with a hug, nearly losing her grip on the cloak in the process. After pulling it back up, she finally spoke, her voice hoarse and raspy.

"Thank you, Lan. You…jumped in after me? That was reckless," she scolded him. He blushed harder and Kryda smiled at him. "I'm proud of you, Lan." At that, he beamed.

* * *

When Eilatra returned with Kryda's breakfast, Kryda was soundly asleep. Eilatra smiled and set the tray down near the tub, placing one hand on Kryda's shoulder to wake her. The dwarf awoke with a start, sloshing water everywhere and completely dousing the candles by the tub, plunging the room into darkness. Eilatra squealed as the water splashed over her, then giggled. Kryda sat up groggily, blinking owlishly in the sudden darkness. Eilatra groped around the room for the candles, but the moment she took a step, she slipped and tumbled into the tub with Kryda, shrieking as she splashed into the water.

"Are ye alrigh'?" Kryda gasped, laughing a little in spite of herself.

"Yes. I hit my head a bit when I fell, but it's not that bad." Eilatra managed, eternally grateful that the darkened room hid her rapidly colouring cheeks.

Kryda managed to retrieve a candle and light it, holding it up to take a look at Eilatra's head. "You're bleedin'. Here." Kryda fished some herbs from the tub, gently patting them into the gash on Eilatra's forehead.

"Thank you. You know some healing?"

"Ah...no, not really. It just, ah, seems like the right thing..." Kryda swallowed, her heart pounding. Eilatra's face was so close to her own. They stayed that way for a moment before Eilatra looked away, laughing nervously. Kryda cleared her throat. "Here, let me help ye get out o' here so you can go get cleaned up."

"Oh, thank you. Um...I left your clothes over there for when you're done. Would you like me to bring anything up to your room later? I just need to go check on Gibbs...he didn't come in tonight."

"Nah, I'll be fine. You go tend to the poor ol' bugger. He's probably needin' a dwarven hangover cure as well. He needs ye more tha' I do." The moment the words escaped her lips, Kryda was kicking herself. *Why would I be sayin' somthin' like tha'? Like I need her at all...* Kryda managed to keep a straight face until the door closed behind Eilatra, then she scoffed at herself and sunk into the bath again, blowing bubbles with the exhale of a deep breath she hadn't realised she'd been holding.

CHAPTER 8

Chapter 9

The Orientation

The next morning, Kryda awoke feeling more refreshed than she'd felt since before she'd even started thinking about leaving her village. The bath had really helped—*why don't we do that back at home?*—and she was excited to meet up with the crew at the Adventurer's Guild. She gathered all of her belongings into her pack and tidied the room a bit, although it was still in nearly perfect order from Eilatra's attentions the day before, and hurried down the stairs.

She ran into Eilatra on the way down—or rather, Eilatra ran into her. The barmaid was in such a hurry that she would have fallen right back down the stairs if Kryda hadn't caught her arm.

"Whoa! Slow down, lass. Ye nearly sent yerself to the healer's hut. What's yer hurry?"

"Oh, nothing," Eilatra replied dismissively, frowning as she noticed the pack on Kryda's back. "You're leaving?"

CHAPTER 9

"Aye, I do be...am off to find me glory in the Adventurer's Guild."

"Right, of course," Eilatra murmured, forcing a smile that didn't quite reach her eyes. "Well, I'm sure I will see you here again with the rest of the crew." She stepped back, tugging her arm from Kryda's grasp and extending her hand for a parting shake, but Kryda pulled her into a hug instead.

"You've been too good to me for a mere shake o' the hands," Kryda insisted. "You be takin' good care o' yerself now, and if ye ever be needin' help with that ol' man o' yers, you just call fer me." Kryda stepped back and smiled at the elf, then continued down the stairs, pausing at the bottom to wave farewell.

Eilatra watched her go, lingering just a little too long after the door closed behind her.

* * *

Kryda had left the tavern earlier than she'd originally planned to, but she was glad she had when she finally crossed the gate into the upper terrace. It was like she'd entered an entirely new city. The terrace wasn't as boisterous as the lower streets of the city; the people who strode through the streets here did so with purpose, and everyone seemed very civil and composed.

The colours of their clothing were much more vibrant as well, and Kryda felt particularly out of place in her plain brown leather tunic. The women all wore shoes with thick soles that added several inches to their height, yet they walked so smoothly that they appeared to float. Their flowing skirts drifted past their feet, yet never brushed the ground, the fabric scarcely even making a sound as they moved.

The smells were different here too. Instead of hearty food, leather, and animals, the air smelled of flowers. Lots and lots of flowers. Kryda stopped to smell some of them, but soon realized that the smells weren't actually coming from the flowers—not entirely, at least. A tall human woman brushed closely past Kryda as if she hadn't even seen the dwarf, and the flowery scent as she passed was so strong that Kryda sneezed violently and stumbled into the rose bush behind her. She scrambled back to her feet, hoping no one had seen, and brushed herself off. As she looked up, she found herself face to face with Captain Harden.

"Are you alright?" he asked, trying to cover his amusement. Kryda hadn't realised that she was so close to the Academy; he must have seen her in the crowd.

"I'm fine. That woman smelled like she'd been rollin' in rose bushes too, which I can tell ye now isnae all that comf'table."

"I hate it when they wear that much perfume," he laughed, wrinkling his nose and smiling at her. "Come on, we'd better get in and report to the Optio. She doesn't like to be kept waiting."

Harden led her through the streets and towards the gates of the Academy. The moment they arrived, Kryda noticed an instant change in Harden. His posture straightened and he became austere all of a sudden, speaking to the guards only in terse, clipped phrases, if at all, and responding to their salutes with curt nods. He said nothing to Kryda until they came to a huge set of doors, with two guards posted in gleaming armour at either side.

"Let me do the talking unless she asks you a direct question," he instructed Kryda, scrutinizing her carefully for a moment. Kryda nodded once and Harden turned back to the guards. "A new recruit to see the Optio."

The guards lifted the beam that latched the doors and pushed them open, just wide enough for Harden to slip inside. Kryda caught a glimpse of him kneeling before a figure seated at a massive desk, the single large window in the rear of the room spilling just enough light around the figure that Kryda could just make out the silhouette. One thing was apparent; the Optio was formidably large.

Harden returned and bid Kryda enter. As the two approached the desk, Kryda's eyes slowly began to adjust to the light. The Optio rose from her chair, towering over both of them—not surprising in Kryda's case, but Harden was not a small man.

"Welcome." The voice was even bigger than the person, reverberating through the room as she spoke. Stepping into the light, Kryda could finally see the source of the booming voice and was pleased to see, for the first time in her life, a female half orc. Her raven-black hair was pulled tightly into a topknot, accentuating the scar slashed across her forehead.

"What brings you to my chambers today, Captain?"

"A new recruit, Optio. I happened upon her two nights ago at the tavern when I arrived to gather my charges. She has travelled a long way."

"So it must be, to have a dwarf among us. What brings *you* here, o young and mighty dwarf?"

Kryda was a bit taken aback at the question. She had expected practical questions regarding her capabilities, not philosophical ones pertaining to her motives. She looked askance at Harden, who gave no indication that he noticed.

"I'm not entirely certain, ma'am," Kryda began. "And I s'pose that's exactly why I've come." The Optio looked down at her thoughtfully, and for a moment Kryda was mildly concerned that she may have given the wrong answer. But then the woman smiled.

"What is your name?"

"Kryda, ma'am."

"Kryda. Very well. Captain Harden here seems to know something of your needs, so I will entrust you to his care for the time being." She turned to face Harden, who nodded his assent.

"She is a beginner, ma'am, and will have her orientation with me today before joining the rest of my crew. Their training has already been arranged for my absence."

"Excellent. You are in good hands, Kryda. Work hard, ask questions, and be sure you are willing to learn from your fellow adventurers. You'll do just fine. Oh, and one more thing. Who sent you here?"

"A kender, ma'am, by the name of Traz."

"I see. Gruck!" An orc even larger than the Optio stepped obediently out of the shadows. *How could I possibly 'ave missed tha'?* Kryda thought. *He's a bloody mountain!*

"Trashj. Shiniez," the Optio grunted, nodding to the massive orc. He snorted in return and melted back into the shadows, but this time Kryda could hear his heavy footfalls and the creak of a back door. The Optio turned back to Kryda. "Off you go now, Kryda. I will check in with you in a few days."

* * *

Harden led Kryda out of the central building and towards the barracks, where Kryda spotted the crew just finishing their breakfasts and beginning their warmups. The moment Kryda and Harden were out of sight of the Optio's guards, Harden dropped his curt, businesslike air and smiled at his trainees.

"Good morning, you lot. Is Connahay not here yet?"

Leeta strolled up to them and clapped a hand down on Kryda's shoulder as she answered. "Not yet, sir. Fine by me! You know what a stick in the mud he is. Come with me, Kryda. I'll show you to the barracks so you can choose a bed." Kryda waved to the rest of the crew as the two of them headed off to the barracks.

Odo approached Harden as he watched them go. "It would seem that our newest member has a certain…allure, wouldn't you say, sir?" he teased.

Harden turned around, expecting to see Connahay—his crew rarely called him 'sir' in the absence of other company—before he realised that Odo was making fun of him.

"What? No! I mean, I think she has some potential, but tha- " He cut himself off, saved from his fumbling explanation by the arrival of the other officer. Harden cleared his throat as the crew formed rank behind him to greet Connahay.

"You're late, Connahay," Harden remarked sharply.

"Please excuse my tardiness, Captain Harden," Connahay replied smoothly. "I had to take care of a minor disturbance at the western barracks this morning." He nodded curtly to the senior Captain before turning to the crew. "Where is Leeta?"

Kurt stepped forward slightly. "She is showing our new recruit around the

CHAPTER 9

barracks, sir."

"Which is where I should be now," Harden interrupted. "G'day, Connahay. I expect a full report of the day on my desk by sundown."

"Yes, sir."

Harden strode towards the barracks, followed by the sound of Connahay hollering orders at his crew as if they didn't practice the same way every day—casters at the practice stone and fighters at the dummies. *Sorry, lads*, he thought to himself, a slight sense of guilt tugging at him. He pounded the door of the barracks, hearing Leeta and Kryda laughing about something or other.

"Leeta, get back out there. Connahay will throw a fit."

"Oh, shit! Is he here now?" She turned to Kryda and extended her hand for a firm warrior's handshake, clasping each other's wrists in camaraderie. "Whoa!" Leeta exclaimed as her fingers closed around the iron-hard leather of Kryda's new bracers. "You'll have to tell me where you got those bracers. Amazing. I'll see you at mess tonight!" She threw Harden a lazy salute before rushing back out to the training grounds. Harden shook his head fondly as he watched her go, then turned and bowed slightly to Kryda, gesturing to the door with an exaggerated flourish.

"Shall we?"

* * *

Harden showed Kryda around the grounds of the Academy, explaining some of the rules and inner workings of the Guild. They visited the armoury, and Kryda tried out a few of the weapons there.

"They're all so light," she remarked, tossing each option from one hand to the next and twirling them about.

"Well, yes. That's usually what a fighter is looking for so they don't wear themselves out. It also helps with speed and agility."

"When it comes to a pick, ye want the tool to do most o' the work for ye. If it were light like these, I'd wear meself out tryin' to break rocks with me own strength."

"Hitting a moving target is different than hitting a rock," Harden cautioned her. "Speed is much more important than strength. And, in any case, living targets are much more fragile than rocks."

They continued on through the eastern quarter and the central building, past the grand doors of the Optio's office, which was located in the eastern quadrant of the central building.

"The Optio, she be second in command, yea? So, where is the Gen'ral's office?"

"Ah, just what we are coming to," Harden replied with a sly smile. He opened a hidden door in the wall beside the Optio's office that Kryda hadn't noticed, and the moment it swung open, the hallway was flooded with light. Kryda had to blink a couple of times to adjust.

They walked through a wide corridor, open to the sky, and into a courtyard overgrown with exotic plants and a pond with a fountain. The statue in the midst of the fountain was a beautiful woman whose race Kryda couldn't quite place. She was too tall for a human, but too short for an elf. Her ears resembled a gnome, but they were much smaller in proportion to her head. Her eyes were covered with a scarf, and with one hand she held a rose to her nose. The other hand clutched a heavy tome. She was obviously a relic, but had been wonderfully maintained.

Around the pond curled a ramp fashioned out of a massive tree trunk, vines curling up its sides as it led up to a small building suspended above the courtyard by great, arched buttresses from each quadrant.

"Each of those supports has a path on top to access the General's office. The only entrances are through the Optios' offices."

"The back doors?"

"Yes. Very few people are permitted up there—or in here—unguarded. The path up there extends overtop the entire central building, so guards and officers can look over the soldiers. That's also how the Optios communicate to each other outside of their regular meetings in the general's hall."

"There're more Optios?" Kryda asked, unused to such complex management.

CHAPTER 9

"Yes, one for each division on city management. The General then reports to the mayor."

Harden briefly checked the position of the sun. "Let's head back over to the training grounds. Connahay should have the crew doing some training outside the walls by now, so we'll have the area to ourselves."

They returned, passing right by the area where they'd met up with the crew earlier, past the practice weapon racks and training dummies and into a serene enclosure, a pulsing crystal standing a good ten feet high in the center. Kryda's mouth was almost watering as she tried to imagine how much a gem like that would be worth!

"How'd they get it in here?" she wondered, mostly to herself.

"This is what we like to call our practice stone. It is actually called a Valanian crystal node. It is said that all the nodes of this crystal are connected to each other and to the Source of all magic which flows through the center of the earth. These nodes help the magic users in their training, and the Academy was built up around them. There is one in each quadrant. Magic users normally have a limit of how much magic they can use before they exhaust themselves. These stones allow them to tap directly into the source instead of draining their personal reserves, so they can practice their spells more often. The closer you are to one, the more you can do. The further away you get, the more you must pull from your personal power and the harder it is to conjure spells. That is why Connahay will have the crew outside the city walls for part of the day. The magic users must get used to relying on their own power, and the fighters will be practicing survival skills like trapping and stealth."

"Have ye ever had 'em hunt from the trees?"

"What?"

"Just a trick I picked up on me journey up 'ere." They headed back out to the fighting area, and while Harden was staring thoughtfully at the rack of practice weapons and trying to decide which weapon to start Kryda on, he heard a loud *thunk* from one of the training dummies. Kryda had flung her pickaxe directly into its chest.

"Yes, yes; we know you can throw your pickaxe at a target like it's filled with gold, but we need to see how you'll do with some of these other weapons." He tossed her a wooden broadsword and squared off with her. "Let's start with stance. See how my legs are spread apart and staggered? That provides stability and maneuverability." Kryda copied the stance. "Good, but less rigid." He pushed her just hard enough that she lost her footing and had to readjust her stance. "Now you push me." She pushed him back—likely harder than was necessary—but he moved with the push and kept his footing. "See how I did that? My legs are ready to move and compensate for whatever forces my body encounter."

"Aye, like a willow."

"Yes, like a willow. What you had there was like an oak. Solid, but brittle and inflexible. A willow is nearly impossible to break because it can almost double over on itself. Now, try swinging at me with the sword." Kryda complied, and Harden dodged the blow easily, but Kryda once again lost her footing, not yet used to the lack of weight.

"Easy, Kryda! You've got strength to spare, there's no doubt about that, but you lack finesse. Maybe we'll try fencing." He took the broadsword from her and turned back to the weapons rack to switch to the rapiers. "This style of swordplay is all about inflicting small slashes that wear your enemy down. It's incredibly annoying to be on the receiving end, but devilishly fun to be on the dealing end."

He handed a rapier to Kryda and jigged fancy little warm-up with his own that looked more like a dance than a fight, but he looked good doing it. He grinned impishly when he finished, rapier pointed at her, one hand poised behind his back.

"Yer specialty, I'd be guessin'?" she asked wryly. He flourished a low bow in response without taking his eyes from hers. She pointed her rapier at him awkwardly.

"Go on and strike," he encouraged her.

She swung the thing up over her head and attacked with a full arm swing. The thin metal bent so far from the force of her swing that Harden didn't even have to dodge; it missed him by a full three inches. While Kryda's shoulder was extended past him and exposed, he flicked his wrist ever so

CHAPTER 9

slightly and whipped her across the shoulder blade.

"GAH! Bloody—" Kryda bit back the curse, straightening back into her position opposite the trainer.

"A sharpened blade would have left a nasty gash, and you'd hardly have felt it. That's how this weapon works. Your enemy doesn't even know how badly he's damaged until he's dizzy from blood loss. Come over here to the dummies and let me show you."

He unsheathed the gleaming rapier he wore on his hip and stood in front of the dummy, utterly still for a moment, before flicking his wrist with lightning speed. Kryda looked at the dummy and thought he'd missed. He knew she'd think that.

"Look more closely," he instructed, smiling. Kryda approached the dummy and ran her hand over the side of it. She found a small slash in the outer fabric and when she pushed on the bundle, she could see that the slice was actually about three inches deep.

"Hit the right spot and your opponent will go down in one swing, but even if you don't get that opening, a few good slashes anywhere will suffice. In an even match, you may only get shallow cuts, but they come fast. That's why the other aspect of this style is training the agility to dodge. Let's just start you on using the sword for now, though."

Kryda brought took her practice rapier to another dummy and raised her arm to swing—not as high as before, she had been listening—but still caused the blade to bend and wobble as she swung at the dummy. Harden came up behind her and tentatively put one hand on her shoulder and the other on her outstretched wrist. "May I?"

Kryda nodded and let him guide her movements. He held her body and shoulder still and showed her to turn the blade in small circles using only her wrist. They practiced slow circles in both directions, then he had her do one small, fast circle in each direction. "Good, now just little flicks - still ONLY using the wrist."

He eased his grip and she started to move from the elbow. He touched her elbow to remind her to hold it still, but let her flick her wrist on her own. Right, left, up, down and again. As she practiced, he had to touch her elbow a few times to remind her not to move it. The blade still wobbled awkwardly after a few rounds, but her elbow was finally still.

"Now I want you to use your whole arm, but only small, even movements for direction, not force. Like a gentle wave." He held her wrist again and showed her the motion only once before taking half a step back and letting her try it on her own. She felt that the wave analogy was apt, and it reminded her of the gentle waves rippling into her secret cave. Holden's hands were still ever so gently guiding her movements, and Kryda closed her eyes to feel the rhythm. "Now, STRIKE!"

All at once, Holden grasped her hand and led her wave to crash into the shoulder of the dummy. The strike landed before she even opened her eyes. Holden stood back and watched Kryda's expression as she looked from the blade to the dummy, which now sported a long slash through its shoulder. It wasn't as clean as Harden's had been, but he'd been using a real blade. The practice blade had done blunt damage to the bundle of straw. Kryda was pleased with the effect, although the gentleness still felt awkward to her. She lowered her arm and immediately grabbed at her shoulder.

"Ugh, why does it hurt like a zap from Thor?" She rubbed the sore muscle, grimacing.

"You're used to using the large muscles for strength, not the fine muscles for control. It will take some time to work them in. Here, let me help." He held her shoulder again and slowly stretched out her arm. As he lowered it again, he pressed the fingers of his other hand into the muscle under her collarbone, inside the socket of her shoulder. Kryda gasped from the pain, but the pressure of his fingers, though uncomfortable, seemed to have eased something in her shoulder when he let go.

"I didnae even know it could hurt there," she muttered. The sun was setting, and Harden stepped back from Kryda as he heard the crew coming back in from the city. Odo, the stealthy bugger, was already within the arena and watching them.

"Welcome back, Odo." Harden shot him a look that dared him to say anything about what he saw, but the halfling just raised both hands in deference with a smile. Kryda didn't notice the exchange, rolling her arm as

CHAPTER 9

she walked back to the weapons rack to replace the rapier. The rest of the crew came barreling through the gate, excited to finally drop their equipment and head out to the tavern for some drinks.

Chapter 10

The Mission

On their way out of the training grounds, Kryda spotted Harden finishing up his briefing with Connahay and waited for him. She invited him to come along with them to the tavern, but he declined respectfully.

"Afraid I can't. I have to stay here and do up some paperwork for the Optio, not to mention making an appearance at the hall with the other officers. Their idea of a party is a single glass of tasteless sparkling grape juice. It's stuffy and insufferable, but I need to at least try to act the part of a Captain." He grinned. "Don't worry, I'll be down to 'collect' you soon enough."

"But ye can't stay then either, or they'll think yer not takin' yer post serious?"

"Something like that, yes."

"Surely ye get some days off, ye poor bastard," she teased him.

"I do…but even then, there are certain things that are still expected of me. Go on without me, Kryda. I'll see you in a couple of hours, and I know the others are getting impatient," he reminded her.

CHAPTER 10

Kryda looked up and noticed that he was right. Kurt and Paddy hadn't seemed to take much notice of them and were chatting idly with each other as they waited, but Leeta was bouncing on the balls of her feet, watching her and Harden impatiently. Kryda also noticed that Odo, who hadn't joined the conversation with Kurt and Paddy, seemed to be pointedly avoiding her gaze. *What'd I do to offend him?* she wondered, but as she did so, Harden clapped her playfully on the back and pushed her towards her friends. Setting that thought to the side, she trotted over to them with a grin, and they headed off.

The crew made their way down the hill towards the tavern, Kryda and Leeta looking half drunk already, catching up on the day and laughing rambunctiously. Kryda was the first through the door of the tavern, and it took her a moment to realise that the rest of the crew had slowed as they came through the doorway, looking much less excited than they had a mere moment ago.

"Wha's the holdup?" Kryda inquired, noting that they were all staring in the same direction. Leeta tilted her chin at a group of heavily armored men across the room.

"That lot are completely guaranteed to ruin our fun," Leeta sneered. Just as she said so, one of them glanced toward the door and pointed out Kryda's crew to his own. They all stood up, their armour clinking and gleaming in the light from the sconces, and swaggered towards the doorway.

"Sorry, this tavern is for *adventurers*, mate," one of the men drawled. Paddy clenched his fists, and Kryda thought she felt his hand growing eerily cold beside her. Leeta stood her ground as the hulking man, who likely had a bit of orc blood somewhere in his line, sauntered near enough for her to smell his breath. She grimaced at the pungent scent. It was obvious that he had used some kind of scented oil to try to cover his halitosis, which only made things worse.

"Oh, really?" Leeta studied her fingernails, picking at them casually. "That's unfortunate, because all I see here are a bunch of glorified attendants in fancy armour who've never seen the inside of a real dungeon. What're you doing down here with us lowly rookies, anyway? Did your Captain ground you for spilling some goats' milk?" Leeta was clearly exacerbating the man's bad temper, and Kryda was nearly certain that she was doing it on purpose. The man spat at Leeta's feet, his face coloring.

"You pond scum haven't even been sent on a mission, never mind a dungeon crawl. You wouldn't be able to afford even *this* dump without riding on the coattails of your fancy famous Captain." Kryda blinked. She had no idea that Harden was famous.

Fankin stepped closer to Leeta and the orcish man. "If that's what you think, then it might interest you to know that we've been tasked with a mission by no less than the Governor of Starting City himself."

"Oh, is that so?" The man laid a hand on his chest and leaned back, his eyes widening with mock wonder. "What's he asked you to do then, eh? Sweep the streets? It'd be a better use of your time than your so-called training."

Leeta stepped forward, her fists clenching, and prepared to swing a fist at his jaw before Kryda stepped in.

"'Ello, sir, me name's Kryda. I'm new to this lovely city an' I'd love to hear a story from a grand adventurer such as yerself!"

The man smiled at her, gratified. "Well, hello there—"

Kryda cut him off. "Did ye ever face an ogre? Take out an army of kobolds, maybe? How about a snow troll?"

"Well, I, uh…"

"Never mind, I'm sure ye'll get to! Yer armour's so shiny! It must take a good deal o' gold to keep it repaired, what with all the dangerous missions ye've 'ad."

"Well, as a matter of fact, we've just returned from a *very* important mission for the King of Human City, wherein we protected a very precious package from bandits on the road!"

"Ooh, bandits ye say? How many of 'em were there? How many'd ye defeat?" Kryda gazed up at him with the eyes of a starstruck child. The rest of her crew were stifling laughter, fully aware that she was mocking him, but trying their best to keep a straight face. The big man looked around at the rest of his men.

"We were fortunate enough to not have need of killing anyone," he said, affecting an air of great and noble mercy.

CHAPTER 10

"How kind of ye! It must be even harder to subdue the scoundrels without killing."

"Why, yes, it certainly is—"

One of his own men interrupted him this time. "We don't leave survivors!" That was the smallest of the men, bigger than Kryda but only by a hand, trying to look tough. He was completely oblivious to the fact that he'd just completely discredited his companion's story. The big guy elbowed him roughly.

"Only when they leave us no *choice*, of course—"

Kryda interrupted again. "Ye musta seen some action, though. Wha's this smudge here, on your breastplate?" She pointed to a spot on his chest and he looked down, confused, as if there were no possible way his breastplate could have been damaged.

"Ach, never mind. It's just what's left of yer pride." Kryda plucked at his breastplate, as if pulling something off, and flung it to the floor. Kurt could no longer contain his amusement and snickered loudly, spurring the rest of the crew to burst out in peals of hysterical laughter. By now, the rest of the tavern had taken notice of the confrontation, and Kryda heard chuckles from several corners of the room.

The humiliated man glanced wildly around the tavern, fully aware that he'd lost any respect he might have had when he walked in. Furious, his jaw clenching, he pushed his way past Kryda's crew and stormed out of the tavern. Some of his men looked like they'd been looking forward to a brawl, but they followed their leader out. As they left, the last one threw a final, furious look around the tavern.

"We don't have to answer to the lot of you!" he shouted, and Kryda could hear him mumbling to himself. She called out the door after them.

"Sorry the pay from yer grand mission weren't enough for a better tavern!"

Those posh pricks must have been universally hated for the whole tavern cheered at their departure. Kryda climbed onto the nearest table and gave a grand bow to the room before following her friends to the recently vacated table.

105

KRYDA'S BEGINNINGS

* * *

The crew didn't have to wait long for Harden tonight. When he finally entered, he seemed more in need of a drink than ever. Eilatra didn't wait for him to order and placed a drink in his hand before he'd even made it to the table.

"What's gotten into you tonight, Harden?" Fankin asked as Harden set down his empty glass.

"Connahay is insufferable! He wants to lead you lot on your mission, since he was the one who was given the order today—even though it's in my name."

"Oh aye, Fankin mention'd tha' earlier. What's it about?" Kryda asked.

"There's something wrong in the sewers. Probably a blocked pipe or something, but there tend to be some nasty critters in there, so they can't send a civilian cleanup crew until it's been scouted. Funny enough, Connahay hates the sewers. He always passed his trainees off to me when he was supposed to take them down there, but now he wants this mission because it was given to *me*. He wants the Optio to think I'm slacking off and he's—"

Harden broke off as Eilatra came 'round with more ale for everyone, and knocked a second mug back so quickly that Paddy passed his own over to Harden and motioned for Eilatra to bring them a few more. Harden took a deep breath, sipping at his third mug of ale.

"How'd ye get down here so fast, anyway?" Kryda prodded him.

"I told the Optio that I had some paperwork I needed to finish up for the Governor regarding the mission—*after* I took the order back from that son of a bitch."

"I thought ye'd finished tha' before we left."

"I did. And now I'm here." Harden smiled for the first time since he'd arrived, raising his glass to the crew, who cheered heartily in response. "You all know I'd rather be here than up there in that stuffy hall."

"So, what's the plan with this mission, then?" Odo asked.

"It'll take a few days to get the details sorted out, but it's a pretty standard run through the sewer system. We make sure there's no critters or beasts

CHAPTER 10

taking up residence down there, and see if we can spot any issues to help send the clean up crew in the right direction. I'll send a couple of you to different areas of the city to monitor the issue and inspect the entrances, so we can get a better idea of where to start. We'll have to wait for the full report from the Governor before we begin, though. That'll give me time to get Kryda up to speed on the basics, and hopefully she should be able to join us. It's a very low level mission, of course, which means we're really not likely to run into anything more than a rat or two."

"What alerted the Governor to the problem?" Leeta leaned forward, sipping her ale.

"Well, the people in the lower circle were complaining of a foul smell from the grates. More foul than normal, I mean." Harden had relaxed now, and he leaned back in his chair, closing his eyes. "Until we receive word from the Governor, we will continue with training, and Kryda will join us in our regular rotation. It's not normally done so fast," he remarked, mostly for Kryda's benefit, then turned back to the others. "But I don't want Connahay anywhere near this, or near any of you, for that matter. You are all capable enough at this point that I can focus my attention mainly on Kryda's training, to help her catch up, but of course I will still be available to you should you need guidance."

The crew began to chat and banter as per their usual shenanigans in the tavern. Eilatra came over to check on their drinks, interrupting a conversation between Leeta and Kryda to ask the dwarf to step aside with her for a moment. Kryda followed her as Eilatra led her to the back door of the tavern.

"I heard that you're going on a mission already?" she asked, her voice trembling slightly.

"Aye, but nothin' glamorous. Just some gross sewer clean up. Grunt work, nothin' real."

Eilatra sighed and closed her eyes tightly, lowering her head and pinching the bridge of her nose between her fingers.

"Wha's wrong, Eilly? Wha's the matter?" Kryda reached up to lay a hand on her shoulder, and the elf straightened suddenly, taking a deep breath.

"Nothing, just… be careful. You've only just arrived, barely even started to train, and something doesn't smell right with this sewer business."

"I know, that's why—"

"No, I mean it. Something is really wrong down there, and people have been getting sick. I—I think it might be related."

"What makes ye say tha'?"

"I don't know, exactly. Call it a woman's intuition."

"Well, alright. I've never had a lick o' the stuff, but me mum had it somethin' uncanny, so I trust that you've got it too, lass. I'll be careful, as ye say."

* * *

Leeta watched curiously as Kryda and Eilatra wandered off toward the back door.

"That seem strange to anyone else?" she asked the group, poking a thumb at the two women, seemingly deep in intense conversation.

"I would not presume to know. We have not known Kryda very long, so how are we to know what is odd?" Paddy shrugged, lifting his glass to his lips.

"We haven't known Kryda long, but have you ever seen Eilatra do that? Take someone aside who wasn't causing a ruckus? She doesn't know Kryda that well, either." Leeta paused as she spotted Kryda heading back to her seat.

"What was that about?" Leeta inquired.

"She's worried about this thing in the sewers. Thinks there might be more to it; a connection to some people getting sick."

"Why would she say that? It's just a stinking sewer." Leeta looked over at Harden, who seemed to be carefully considering Eilatra as he rolled his empty mug idly around on the table.

"I've seen Eilly do that before," he remarked. "Closing her eyes and pinching her nose. I think she gets some kind of visions. I've asked, and she'll never admit to anything special about herself, but she's been right before about

CHAPTER 10

sensing danger. I think I'll do some digging on these illnesses."

* * *

When Eilatra arrived at their table with the next round, she pulled Kryda aside again.

"Kryda, I hate to ask you this, but...could you please go check on Gibbs for me? I haven't seen him since the other night, which is odd; he's here every night usually. I'm really worried about him, but I can't leave the cook on his own on such a busy night."

"O' course ah will. No worries, lass, ah'm sure he's fine. Ah'll be back in two shakes o' the flask."

Kryda told Harden and the crew what Eilatra had asked of her. "Go ahead," Harden encouraged her. "We'll be here a bit yet." Her Captain's permission gained, Kryda headed down the road to Gibbs' run-down estate and knocked lightly on the red door. When there was no response, she tried the knob, and found that it was unlocked. She opened it just a crack and peered inside.

"Oi, Gibbs," Kryda called into the dark house. Her voice echoed through the empty halls. "Ye there, mate?" There was no reply. She thought of turning out and telling Eilatra that he wasn't home, but then she heard a faint shuffling noise upstairs. She slowly entered the house and crept up the stairs, remembering Harden's insistence on trusting Eilatra's intuition.

The upstairs was a mess. She stepped carefully over empty bottles and dodged piles of old parchment and fresh scribbled notes, trying to move as silently as she could. Following the sounds of the shuffling and rustling of papers, she found herself outside a study, the door cracked open slightly. She peered inside to see Gibbs hunched over a desk covered in papers and candles. *No' the safest o' plans,* Kryda thought to herself wryly. She waited a moment before announcing herself, just to be sure there was no one else there.

"Gibbs? Are ye alright there, ol' man?"

Gibbs' head jerked up from his papers, but it took a moment for his mind to return to the present and recognise his new friend. "Kryda! Oh yes, yes, I'm fine. Do come in. Maybe you can help me with this. Here." He picked the piece of parchment he'd been staring at and passed it over to her, then turned to squint at some parchments he'd plastered to the wall, holding a candle to them for light—dangerously close to the highly flammable pages.

Kryda looked down at the hastily scrawled words. "It's a list o' names."

"Precisely, miting." Kryda winced at the term of endearment. Gibbs noticed and grinned at her. "If you can call me 'old man', then I get away with calling you 'miting', miting." Kryda grumbled, but decided to indulge him.

Gibbs gestured to the list she held. "The first name there is the most recent in a string of suspicious deaths. I've been telling everyone for ages...there's something going on here. They all just looked at me like I was crazy! Well, I was—I was crazy with grief—but that isn't the point. I'm more convinced than ever that I'm right. I was coming in by the back door earlier when I overheard you talking to Eilly about them sewers. I know what it means when she shudders like that. She *knows* something."

He shook off that thought and pointed at the list again. "I'd given that up for awhile, but after I heard what she said, I came straight back here to make a new list, including the most recent deaths."

"These dates...they go back months!" Kryda gasped, scanning the page. The final entry was dated two years prior. "Two years...that's...yer wife. She was the first death, wasn't she? Yer son the next?"

Gibbs bowed his head. "Yes. That's what started all this." He gestured around the room. "It's also why no one took me seriously. Eilly, bless her, was the only one who even humoured me. I doubt she believed me either, but at least she was kind to me. She just didn't think it was healthy for me to get obsessed the way I do. I think I may have something this time, though! I have to go check it out—it'll take me a couple of days to prepare—would you come with me?" he stammered excitedly, looking over at Kryda with such a gleam of hope in his eyes that she was caught completely off guard.

"O'course I will, if I can...but, ah..ah'm supposed to be goin' with the crew in a couple of days. Ah'll need to have a wee chat with Harden, I suppose...

CHAPTER 10

but it sounds like it might be related an' he said he wanted to gather more information. I think he'll allow it."

Gibbs was so delighted that it seemed to Kryda as if he'd shed twenty years. "Wonderful! You go back and have a chat with him, then, and meet me back here."

"Wha—tonight?? I thought you said it would take you time to prepare."

"Well, yes, but it'll take you some time to prepare as well! You need to go over all of this." He turned back to face the parchments, looking them over with pride. "I've got nearly two years worth of obsession driven research in here."

"Alright, I'll stop by for a bit before we go back up to the Academy, but I still have trainin' to do. Gather some scrolls that I can take with me, if ye like."

"Right, right. Yes. That will do. Oh, and Kryda…don't tell Eilly, please? She'll be over here in an instant, distracting me with her worrying while I'm trying to concentrate, trying to get me to eat and get outside in the fresh air. BAH! I'll get plenty of fresh air while I'm hunting this mystery!"

"Alright, ol' man. Ah'll tell her yer alright. She's worried sick, ye know…I don't think she'll believe me. Ah think you should go see the lass."

"Yes, I suppose you're right. Why don't I bring the scrolls to you at the tavern, then?"

"Tha' would be better. Then ye can tell Harden about yer plan yerself."

Chapter 11

The Urgrosh

Harden stood in front of his crew, hands clasped behind his back, barking orders. "Alright, you lot, the next couple of days are going to be intense training to prepare for our mission. Today, you will be staying within the training grounds and pushing yourselves to your limits. Tomorrow you will be outside the walls doing the same. Casters, start with a meditation at the crystal, then practice with your highest levels spells until you burn out. Take a rest, then continue with potions and finally the agility course. Make sure you can escape anything that comes at you to keep yourself in the rear, should anything slip past the front line or ambush you. Fighters, start with a warm-up on the obstacle course. Then, I want you to stack your target bales to get ready for weapons training. Once you're warmed up, get in some sparring with your weapon of choice, then hit the books. We'll not neglect our minds, lads, especially when preparing for a job. Make sure you go over the maps of the sewers thoroughly, and mark the entrances on your own maps of the city. Kryda, you and I will start with a quick warm-up, and then you'll spend the entire day on weapons training. I've already seen that you have the raw strength, so our focus today will be to help you find your preferred weapon. Good luck, crew; dismissed."

The adventurers saluted their Captain, then split off to their assigned tasks. Kryda turned to Harden for further direction.

"Wha's first, Cap'n?"

"We'll go run some laps to start, and then I'll see how you do over a portion of the obstacle course."

"Alright. Lead the way."

As they reached the track, Kryda took off across the packed earth, eager to get started.

"Pace yourself!" Harden called, but the advice fell on deaf ears. He shook his head with a smile and followed her onto the track at a jog. By the time Harden had reached the halfway mark, Kryda caught up to him, laughing as she lapped him. By the time he'd reached the starting point again, she was winded, and he caught up to her easily.

"I tried to tell you to pace yourself," he chuckled, keeping pace with her as they jogged.

"How...are ye...talkin'...so easy?" she gasped.

It was his turn to laugh now. "Don't stop!" he encouraged her. "Take it slow until I catch you again, then try to keep pace with me. Just keep going!" Harden sped back up to his brisk, measured pace, while Kryda struggled on. She'd always been a good runner, but only back in her small village, where she was always sprinting around and rarely had reason to run for a long distance. She still hadn't quite caught her breath when Harden made his way back around and spurred her into a steady jog again.

"How many rounds...are we doin'?"

"Two more. Don't talk if it's too difficult."

"Och! I dunnae...think..."

"I said, don't talk."

The rest of the lap was a struggle for Kryda, but by the time they came around for the last lap, she had pushed past the pain and fallen into a good

CHAPTER 11

pace. Harden watched her, bemused, as she reached the starting point again and blew by it without even noticing. He continued alongside her without a word. About halfway through the extra lap, Kryda finally snapped out of her thoughts and realized she'd started an extra lap. She started to slow as she looked over at Harden, suddenly feeling very, very tired again.

He grinned at her. "Race you!"

Harden took off, and as exhausted as Kryda was, she was hardly going to let him run off by himself. She stumbled as she kicked herself back into a sprint. They rounded the course one more time, and as they crossed the starting point again, Kryda collapsed.

Harden joined her, flopping down to the grass and laughing. Well, Harden was laughing. Kryda was mostly coughing.

"You did well. You'll do even better, once you learn not to burn yourself out on the first lap. Let's rest for a moment, and then we'll go get some water."

They lay there for a short while, catching their breath—or at least, so Kryda could catch her breath—and then headed to the obstacle course. Kryda made it through without much difficulty, if slowly, wincing at the pain starting in her legs from the run. Harden praised her for her agility and reflexes. After a quick break for lunch, they started practicing with weapons.

Every weapon Kryda tried just felt *wrong* in her hands. Even the rapier she'd done fairly well with the night before didn't show any further promise. She even tried a bow, hoping that after watching Marcus' expert handling of the weapon, she may have picked up even the smallest inkling of how to use it. But even that last-ditch option proved unsuccessful. After working with various weapons all afternoon, Harden was beginning to wonder if he would simply have to help Kryda adapt her pickaxe skills for combat. He motioned to her to set the weapons down and follow him.

"They're just all too light!" Kryda complained, as they walked back to Harden's office. "I canae get a feel fer somethin' that feels like nothin'!"

"Well, I don't know what else to try, Kryda. Maybe there's something we can do with the pick. Perhaps I'll ask the Optio if she has some heavy orcish weapons still." He sat down at his desk and started searching through some parchment scrolls. When he looked back up, he noticed that Kryda was not paying attention to him at all. She was staring at a weapon hanging on the wall that looked like it had come from another age. It had an axe blade on one side, a curved pick on the other, and a broad, bladed spear tip gracing the head of its long handle.

"Wha's tha'?" she asked, her accent thick with wonder.

"That...is an Urgrosh," Karden told her, standing up from his desk and going to join her in front of the weapon. "I hadn't even thought of this...they were used by the dwarves that used to occupy the area to the south of here, many generations ago. They were great warriors—not so much concerned with gathering as most of the dwarven tribes are now. Their prowess in battle allowed them to explore dangerous places that held great wealth."

He didn't think it possible, but Kryda's eyes widened even further. The childlike awe in her gaze was strangely charming. "Would you like to hold it?" he asked, frankly a little surprised that she hadn't already taken it down herself. She was not exactly the type to wait for permission when she wanted something. *It is mounted pretty high up*, he thought, noting how far back she had to tilt her head to look up at it.

Karden's question shocked Kryda out of her reverie. She stepped back and crossed her arms in a clumsy attempt at indifference. "It certainly looks like a fine piece o' work. Aye, I'd like tae take a closer look, if yer offerin'." Her air of nonchalance was so affected that Harden had to chuckle, but Kryda took no notice.

Harden stepped forward and removed the weapon from the wall, the muscles in his arm tightening against his sleeve as he did so—a testament to the weight of the weapon. Kryda felt her cheeks flush red, not entirely sure if she was blushing over the weapon or the man—perhaps a bit of both. At this point, she was used to seeing him swing around that dainty little thing he called a rapier. She wished he would use something heavier more often, except that if he did, Kryda had to admit to herself that it would probably make it a little difficult for her to concentrate on lessons.

He passed her the weapon, presenting it to her as if it were a newly forged sword, the weapon balanced on the ends of his strong, nimble fingers. She took the weapon from him, all the while returning every bit of reverence he

CHAPTER 11

had shown and tipping her head to return the bow. She turned the weapon over in her hands, delighted with the heft of it. She tested her hands on the grip, lightly tilting the Urgrosh from side to side to assess the balance. Despite its age, it still seemed in very good condition, with not a single chip nor scratch anywhere on it. Laughing joyfully, she twirled the weapon, swinging and jabbing with each built-in weapon, getting a feel for all of them.

"I need to find me one o' these!" Kryda beamed at Harden, finally satisfied with how the weapon felt in her hands and how it made her feel.

"Urgrosh have been very rare since the battle clans were wiped out, and this metal is even more rare. They used to mine it from the mountains to the west, but no one has survived venturing over there since the War of the Scourge."

"I'll be gettin me some one day," she exclaimed, "and I'll have the best Urgrosh ever made!"

Harden smiled at her enthusiasm. "This one is a relic, belonging to one of the founders of the academy. It has been on display in this office for generations." He reached out for the weapon, and Kryda reluctantly passed it back to him. "For now, you'll have to make do with a more basic metal and a human blacksmith. We're not as good as they were," he admitted, motioning to the Urgrosh to indicate the warrior dwarves, "but we've come a long way in the last couple of centuries." He opened a chest in the corner behind his desk and pulled out a pouch, tossing it to Kryda. She caught it against her breastplate with a *clink*—it was a large pouch of silver coins.

"That should be enough for the blacksmith," Harden told her. He quickly drew up a sketch of the Urgrosh and made some notes on the parchment, then rolled it up and handed it to Kryda.

"He's going to look at you like you're crazy, you know…we spent generations refining our metals for light weaponry, and now you'll come along asking for something made from an alloy used only for cauldrons and, well, pickaxes," he laughed, motioning toward the one on her hip. "It'll be heavy enough for you, though. That I can promise. Go now and tell him to hurry—I want it in your hands by tomorrow night. We'll see how your weapon training goes with that. In the meantime, you might as well work on your hand to hand combat sparring. You've got great reflexes when you're in immediate danger, but otherwise…you're mostly just a hazard." She snorted and swatted at him, but he leaped out of the way, still laughing.

Chapter 12

The Old Man

Kryda delivered the Urgrosh sketch to the blacksmith, who did indeed look at her like she'd sprouted several extra heads. "This is definitely going to take some time," he told her, skeptical.

"I've got important business to get to, so we be needin' it right away. The faster ye can finish, the better. Isn't there anythin' ye could do tae speed the process along?"

"I'm sorry, but I'm afraid it's going to take a few days at the least. I don't even have the materials here right now—I'll have to purchase some. Not much use for that kind of metal here these days, I'm afraid."

Kryda grumbled, but she knew there was no way to speed the blacksmith along—she'd just have to make do with her pickaxe for the time being. She handed over the silver coin and thanked him for his time. He had agreed to the job, at least, and had told her that he was honoured she'd ask him to replicate a weapon made by her people, even if it would be a rather crude substitute. Of course, the bag of silver she'd handed him hadn't hurt either.

After leaving the blacksmith, Kryda made her way to Gibbs' house, to return the scrolls she'd read and to glean more information from the old man. Once again she found him in his study, hunched over the documents that littered his desk. Kryda's heart lurched with pity, and she felt a sudden desire to free the old man from his self-imposed confinement.

"Come on out to the tavern wi' me, Gibbs," she coaxed him. "Eilatra'll be glad to see ya, an' we can tell Harden more about your concerns." Gibbs hesitated for a minute, glancing around at the mountains of information piled in his study. "Ye've been over this stuff too many times, Gibbs. Ye need some new eyes to give ye a fresh look."

"Oh, all right. We can talk there, but only if you promise you won't tell Eilly what we're up to!"

"Ye've got a deal, ol' man. We'll act all casual-like when she comes over, aye?"

"Sounds fair enough to me, miting," Gibbs replied, smiling. "Let's go, then!"

Unfortunately, when they arrived at the tavern, Eilatra immediately suspected that the two were up to something. *I'll play along for now,* she thought, *but I may have to follow them later to find out what's going on.* She watched them as they sat deep in earnest conversation in Gibbs' usual corner of the tavern, but when they finally parted ways for the night as they left the inn, she was satisfied that whatever they had up their sleeves was not going to take place that evening.

* * *

Kryda arrived at Gibbs' house early the next morning.

"Alright, ol' man. Let's git goin'!"

Gibbs chuckled fondly at her enthusiasm. "Now, now, miting, I'm coming! I just wanted to find...ah! Here it is." He sprang lightly down the stairs with the energy of a man half his age, brandishing a handful of tattered old scrolls.

CHAPTER 12

"These are my notes from the incident before the deaths of my dear wife and son; and these," he continued, handing Kryda another scroll, "are my thoughts from afterward." Kryda skimmed the documents quickly, her eyes widening as she read Gibbs' description of the sickness in question.

"Ye say yer wife an' son were attacked by a diseased sewer rat that was actin' strange…did it seem larger than usual? And did it look like it was gettin' stronger the more ye fought it?"

"Yes! The damned thing just wouldn't die! I was wearing armour, of course, and so was my boy. We were attempting to kill it, but it was unnaturally quick, the bastard! My wife stood behind us and watched for a few moments, but then she suddenly jumped in front of my boy, just as he was about to bring his sword down on the accursed animal. She grabbed the rat, and it bit and scratched at her. I shouted at her to let it go so we could kill it, but she held on, refusing to let us take it from her. 'Twas nearly the size of a cat, but it seemed smaller in her arms, odd enough, and after a time it seemed to stop struggling. She was crying when she finally let it go, and after a moment I saw that she had done with her little dagger what the boy and I had failed to do with our mighty swords."

Tears began to form in Gibbs' eyes, and he rubbed his worry-wrinkled forehead with one hand as he sighed. "Her scratches became terribly inflamed, and she fell ill almost immediately. The only thing she said about the incident before she died was that she wept for the creature, not for herself; and that we shouldn't either, once she was gone. I thought it was over, when she finally passed, but I didn't know 'till it was too late that my son had gotten a scratch, too. He became so angry…I thought that he was just upset at himself for the death of his mother and that was all there was to it, but then he became so hateful of everyone. He just *burned* with hatred; nothing like the quiet, gentle boy I'd raised. His death was horrible; he passed delirious with fever, raving and ranting about evil and darkness. After seeing some others with minor scratches from household vermin go through similar madness before their deaths, I became convinced that there was more to it than just illness from infected wounds. I often wondered if I'd been affected as well. I searched frantically for the smallest scratches, and never found any; but still, I waited for death. I just wanted to be reunited with my family." Gibbs finally broke down and wept, his shoulders shaking as he sobbed, his head in his hands. Kryda didn't know what to say. She merely reached up to lay a hand on the old man's shoulder, and bowed her head as she cried. Feeling the understanding warmth in her touch, Gibbs took a deep breath, wiping the tears from his eyes and clearing his throat. "You believe me, don't you?"

Kryda nodded. "I do, at tha'. I've seen a creature, slain it, as ye've described. Was even wounded, but I 'ad no hatred in me tae fuel the sickness, and I 'ad the help of a very special healer, along with the love an' kindness of an entire village. One little girl in particular sang wi' me, and filled me heart with enough love that there weren't room left fer darkness."

Gibbs studied her intently, a spark of hope kindling in his tear-bright eyes. "You survived the sickness? I was beginning to think that wasn't possible. We need to solve this puzzle, Kryda. Our meeting was fortuitous! We can save the city...no, we *will* save the city!" he cried. Kryda grinned fondly at his use of grand language, having noticed this tendency of his whenever his hopes were high or his interest piqued.

"Aye, that we will, old man."

Delighted, Gibbs strode to the door, eagerly beckoning Kryda to follow. They headed out together, making their way toward the northern gates of the city.

"And where, might I ask, would the two of you be sneaking off to so early?"

The calm in Eilatra's tone did nothing to soften the sudden start of guilt they both felt at having been caught. Kryda turned and saw that Eilatra had traded her usual tavern dress for a full set of leather armour, as if prepared for an adventure. Kryda flushed and averted her eyes, but Gibbs bowed with charismatic flair.

"Good morning, my dear! We are just out for a morning stroll—"

"Don't you try to Charm *me*, Gibbs. You know I can see right through you. Is this about your wife and son again? You've been acting very strange of late—" she paused and looked pointedly at Kryda, "—and I can see that you've even recruited Kryda into your obsession. I thought she, at least, might have

CHAPTER 12

known better."

Gibbs looked very disconcerted that his smooth attempts at deceit had absolutely no effect on the half-elf.

"But he's not crazy, Eilly," Kryda broke in. "He finally told me the full story, an' I've *seen* what he's been lookin' fer. I've lived it. I can *help* him."

Eilatra looked at her curiously, studying her for a moment. Finally, she sighed, defeated. "Is that so? Well, Gibbs, it seems you've finally got a real lead in your mystery after all. Let's follow it, then, shall we?"

"You want to come with us?" Gibbs spluttered. "But—but—you hated when I got on about this!"

"I hated when it *consumed* you, Gibbs," she told him, gently. "I always believed you; I never thought you were crazy, I just didn't want to let this mystery destroy you when the answers you sought were clearly nowhere to be found. Now that we have something real to follow…things have changed, haven't they? Come along, then!" She smiled brightly, and motioned for Gibbs to lead the way. After a brief moment wherein he continued to stare, gaping, the new reality finally seemed to sink in, and he brightened immediately.

"Well, then, if that's settled at last, we've delayed long enough!" he declared, and turned to lead the way once again. The three of them made their way through the bustling city streets and out the northern gates, then past the few farm houses scattered on the outskirts, Gibbs leading them down a quieter but still well-traveled road before turning onto an overgrown old road.

"This is where it happened," he said, pointing just up the road. "It didn't make any sense to me at the time…"

"Nah, it wouldnae. Naht here. There's hardly any forest 'ere a'tall."

"But there's an outlet for the sewers near here," he remarked, pointing up a hill, back towards the city. "We should start by looking up that way. There's an old entrance up there that most people don't remember; I found it on an old map of the tunnels. There used to be a handful of houses up there, but they all relocated within the gates during the Great War."

Eilatra headed further up the old road, and started searching along the bank of the hill Gibbs had indicated. She plucked a very sickly looking weed

123

and held it up for the other two to see. "I know this area isn't exactly rich with vegetation to begin with, but this looks particularly unhealthy," she noted.

"Tha'd be what we're lookin' fer," Kryda confirmed. "Let's head further up tae where Gibbs' map shows an entrance to the sewers, an' see if there's more up there."

As they headed up the slope, it became more and more obvious that they were moving in the right direction. The sparse vegetation began showing signs of rot that were uncharacteristic for this elevation and climate. It almost felt as if they had entered a bog.

By the time they reached the sewer entrance, their feet began to sink and stick in the muck, and the stink was so intense that it smelled like they were already in the sewer itself. The rank stench emanating from the actual sewer was so overwhelming that Eilatra refused to go any closer than was absolutely necessary to confirm the existence of this entrance. It didn't help that the group could hear all manner of foul creatures skittering around in there as well.

"Anythin' that can live in there has *got* to be unnatural!" Kryda joked, waving a hand in front of her nose.

"We should get back and tell the crew," Gibbs decided, his mouth set in a grim line. "I think your mission may have just gained a few ranks. Your team will need to be prepared."

CHAPTER 12

13

Chapter 13

The Sewers

When Kryda met back up with her crew after the little side quest she'd had with Gibbs, they briefed her on the status of their mission in the sewers. They had already managed to clear the main entryway of some unsavoury vermin, but had yet to discover the source of the problem. Kryda relayed the information she had gathered with Gibbs, as well as their suspicions regarding the recent deaths in the city, and the story of her dealings with the infected boar. Her crew seemed both disturbed and intrigued by her findings, perhaps secretly hoping that if the problem were more serious than they'd initially anticipated, they may gain even more recognition for their first mission than they'd previously hoped.

The team headed back into the sewers together. Kryda was once again overwhelmed by the stench, falling behind as the others made their way through the first section as easily as if it were a stroll through the woods.

"Ach! How can ye all be walkin' through here like i's nothin'?" she

CHAPTER 13

complained. They all paused and looked at her, finally noticing that she'd fallen behind. Fankin scoffed at her.

"If you think this is bad, wait 'till we get through there!" he warned her, gesturing towards the door that lay ahead.

"I canae wait." Kryda replied, rolling her eyes and plugging her nose.

But as they opened the first door, the stench forced all of them to stand back for a moment. Kryda made a particularly big fuss about it, exclaiming and waving her free hand around her face. Kurt patted her on the back, laughing at her through his shallow breathing.

"Why do you think we didn't get any further before?" he chuckled.

"Can we just be tellin' the Governor tha' we didnae find anythin'?" Kryda pleaded with her crew.

"We could, but then we wouldn't get paid," Leeta said dryly.

"Ach! Alrigh' then. Let's be gettin' on with it!" Kryda forced down her reluctance along with the bile that rose in her throat, and was the first to step through the door. Leeta followed her, and the light from the blazing torch in her hand caught something glimmering on the wall near the doorway. Kryda noticed the brief shine, and studied it carefully as the others filed in. The rest of the crew went to examine the pile of bones that lay in the middle of the room, an old rusty sword standing upright in the middle of the heap.

Kurt went straight for the sword, but it was embedded solidly in the stonework. As he tried to wiggle it free, Paddy noticed movement among the bones. Expecting to see a rat or some other sewer creature emerge, he poked at the pile with the butt of his staff. As he did so, it quickly became clear that the movement was not caused by a rat. The small bones near Kurt's foot reformed into a hand and arm and reached for his leg.

"Kurt! Look out!" cried Paddy. Kryda turned from the wall she was studying and sprang into action, leaping forward and bringing her pickaxe down on the elbow joint of the reformed arm, in an attempt to stop the next bone from connecting.

Fankin began to mutter under his breath, preparing a spell as more bones came together and formed themselves into a one-armed skeleton on the other side of Kurt. The skeleton tottered on its feet for a moment, then swung at Kurt, wielding a sword that seemed to have mysteriously appeared from nowhere—a sword that looked almost exactly like the one in the floor. The skeleton missed its swing, however, as Kurt danced around, attempting to shake off the arm that was clutching his leg.

Paddy reached into his bag, pulling out a vial of holy water to throw at the skeleton, but the vial was almost empty. When it shattered open on the floor, it emitted nothing more than a small puff of smoke, but it did manage to get the skeleton's attention. Kurt finally shook off the undead arm clutching his leg as the rest of the skeleton turned on Paddy.

The newly freed arm dragged itself forward with the tips of its bony fingers, walking itself to the other side of Kurt and beginning to climb its way up the rest of the skeleton. But before it could snap itself back into its socket, Odo flung a dagger at the arm with deadly precision. He pinned it expertly to the far wall of the room, the dagger embedded neatly between the two bones of the forearm.

Kryda positioned herself behind the skeleton, swinging the broad side of her pickaxe at its head. The pickaxe connected with a sharp crack, popping the skeleton's head right off its spine. The head clattered to the floor, spinning round and round like a top until it finally came to a stop.

The crew of adventurers stood at the ready, waiting for the skeleton to make another move, but it collapsed to the floor upon the loss of its undead noggin. Fankin released his spell anyway, a fireball spitting from his cupped hands and charring the bones as they fell. The stench became nearly unbearable for a moment, then slowly lifted as the bones hissed away into ash.

The adventurers all sighed in relief, but Fankin began to conjure another spell.

"What're ye at, Fankin?" Kryda inquired.

"I want to know what's going on with that sword," he muttered absently, talking mostly to himself. Kurt returned to the sword, which had previously appeared worn and rusted, but now looked to be in pristine condition. He pulled it easily from the stone floor and brought it to Fankin, who reached his hands toward the weapon, bright magic spilling from his palms and swirling around the blade.

CHAPTER 13

"It doesn't seem to have any special abilities, per se, but it is a magical item," Fankin remarked, as he passed his hands over and around the rest of the sword. "Perhaps a simple glamour to keep it in such a perfect condition. I believe that the state of rot it appeared to be in earlier, as well as the emergence of the skeleton, were part of a separate enchantment." Idly twirling his fingers around the magic swirling in his palms, Fankin began to pass it over the rest of the room, tendrils of misty light reaching out to gently brush the walls as he inspected the area.

They searched the room thoroughly, but found no evidence of more magical objects. When they had finished, they approached the far door, preparing to head deeper into the sewers. Leeta nodded to Kurt, who grinned at her, then lunged forward and rammed his shoulder into the door. It rattled, bits of dirt and rotten wood crumbling to the floor, but held firm. Kurt winced and rubbed his shoulder, stepping back in bewilderment.

"There's no way a door that old and rotten should be that solid," he groaned, looking apologetically at the rest of the crew. Kryda pushed him lightly aside.

"I'll be handlin' this, then," she boasted, strutting across the room and charging at the door, slamming into it full-force like a battering ram. The door didn't budge, and Kryda was flung unceremoniously onto her rump. The crew howled with laughter, but Leeta only tilted her head curiously. Stepping forward, she jiggled the ancient handle, and after a few moments, the door creaked open. Kurt and Kryda both darkened with embarrassment as they realized they'd been trying to break down a door that wasn't even locked in the first place.

"Kurt! Ye didnae even check the damned thing first??" Kryda stared accusingly at her teammate.

"Neither did you!" he retorted, still rubbing his injured shoulder, possibly hoping to soothe his wounded dignity as well.

"Well, forgive me for assumin' ye had enough sense in ye to at least check it before ye tried to bash it!" she cried.

Odo rolled his eyes. "Forget it, you two! What if it had been trapped, anyway? We didn't check for traps either! All of us should have known better," he continued, glancing pointedly at Leeta. The crew murmured in agreement, and Kurt sighed, then reached out a hand to help Kryda up.

With the brief argument ended, the crew proceeded into the next room. The smell was just as bad, but this time it was different: instead of death and sewer-muck, it stunk strongly of *animal*. Kryda took a few hesitant steps into the room, her eyes adjusting to the dark. The room was supported by two rows of pillars in various states of disrepair, fallen chunks of stone littering the floor. The room seemed clear of potential threats, though, so Kryda waved the others in. Leeta followed, holding out her torch. The crew spread out and began to search this room as well.

"Looky here!" Leeta called, a grin on her face. "I call dibs!" She reached down and picked up a severed kobold arm, giggling maniacally. Kryda rolled her eyes and snatched the arm from Leeta, then smacked her with it playfully.

"Ugh, gross!" Leeta laughed, pushing Kryda away. She wiped spattered gore from her arm, then darted forward and smeared it across Kryda's face. "Oh no! Looks like you got some on you, too!" she teased.

"That'll come back to bite yer arse," Kryda grumbled, wiping irritably at her face.

Leeta paused suddenly, lifting her torch higher. "Shhh! Everyone! Listen!"

The alarm in her voice hushed the crew instantly, and a deep silence fell over the room. Then, a low, rumbling growl slowly rose from the far side of the room. Kryda seized Leeta's arm as she spotted a massive, tan-coloured creature lurking in the shadows. It resembled a large cat, but its head was shaped differently. It prowled around the group as Kryda quietly described what she saw to the rest of the crew, who remained still as statues.

"Fankin," Kryda hissed. "Can ye talk to it?"

The gnome closed his eyes, attempting to communicate with the creature, but quickly opened them and shook his head. Kryda watched as the creature melted back into the shadows.

"I cannae see it now," she warned them. "But it's still 'ere."

The crew unsheathed their weapons and stood at the ready, glancing nervously around the room. Unseen, the creature padded silently up a pile of rubble. Alerted by a slight noise, Kryda glanced up and saw it. Just as she did so, the creature shrieked: a high, piercing cry magnified tenfold

CHAPTER 13

by the confines of the room. The adventurers stumbled backwards, their ears ringing. Odo was the first to recover; he clambered up a small pile of crumbling stone and fired his crossbow, missing the creature by a hair.

Kryda could now see that it closely resembled a hyena—a hyena the size of a workhorse. She fell backwards when it screamed, and Leeta and Paddy scrambled forward, helping her back to her feet and dragging her away from the creature as Odo's arrow whizzed past its head. It had not yet noticed Fankin, who was creeping up behind it, but as the creature was startled by the arrow, it whirled around, its tail whipping the gnome to the ground.

The creature leaped at Odo, who dove to the side just in time to avoid its extended claws. Kryda shouted at it, trying to bring its attention away from the rogue, and ducked down as it sprang at her.

Spotting an opportunity, Kurt seized the beast's tail as it jumped past him, and it whirled on him, teeth snapping. As it snarled, Fankin scrambled back to his feet, reciting another spell. His hands ignited as he prepared to release a fireball, but just as he did so, the creature pulled free from Kurt's grasp and lunged, pinning Fankin to the ground. It screeched in pain as Fankin instinctively threw up his flaming hands to protect his face, searing the beast's flesh as he did so. Wounded, the creature released Fankin and whirled back upon Kurt, sinking its fangs into his calf. The beast dragged Kurt to the ground, gnawing on his leg as the warrior howled in pain.

Seeing the creature mauling his companion, Odo dove forward with a shout, plunging his dagger deep into its hindquarter. The creature released Kurt and whirled around to confront its attacker, but the rogue had vanished.

As the beast was distracted, Fankin rolled over to Kurt, who was moaning in pain, and grabbed the wounded man's leg, gasping out a quick healing spell. Desperately trying to keep the beast away from her injured companion, Leeta leaped up from where she had been crouching beside Kryda and waved her torch at the creature, shouting as she did so. Blinded by the flame and still fearful from its earlier burns at the hands of Fankin, it reared up and stumbled backwards, crashing into a pillar. Huge chunks of stone crumbled down, clattering to the floor around Kurt, who rolled over, instinctively sheltering the much smaller Fankin from the debris.

As the beast reared up, distracted by Leeta's flame, Paddy stepped forward and dropped his staff, ice crusting over his fists, sharp points extending from his hastily-formed spiked gauntlets with a cold crackle. He rushed at the beast, plunging into a slide and skidding beneath its belly as he swung one icy fist, connecting directly with the creature's singed face. The weight of the punch flung the creature to the side, knocking it off its feet, its claws digging into the stone floor with a hideous grating as it tried to recover its balance.

The moment it recovered, it sprang at Paddy, but Odo reappeared from the shadows, knife extended, slicing cleanly across the tendons of its rear leg as it leaped. The moment the beast landed, Leeta brought her torch down on its spine, dealing a glancing blow. Dazed and limping, it turned desperately towards Leeta, swiping at her with one massive paw and snarling.

As her teammates harassed the beast, Kryda glanced at the pillars lining the room and had an idea. Scrambling up the one nearest the beast as if it were a tree, she pulled her pickaxe from her belt. As she did so, Odo darted around to the other side of the beast, cutting open the wiry tissue of its other rear leg. The creature collapsed, and Kryda dropped like a stone, one curved edge of her pickaxe sinking deep into its skull with a dull *thud*.

The beast's last snarl died away, blood drooling from its lips, its eyes frozen in a sightless stare. For a moment, the room was silent except for the heavy breathing of the adventurers. Then Kurt, still clutching his wounded leg, raised a ragged cheer. Relieved, the rest of them joined in; all but Kryda, who began circling the beast, anxiously inspecting it for signs of the disease. When the crew realized what she was doing, they became somber again and inspected their wounds, remembering Kryda's warning of the danger posed by even the slightest sign of infection.

Fortunately, they had nothing to worry about—Kryda noticed that the beast's body remained the same size as it had in life, and the blood oozing from its wounds was a deep red, not the thick, sickly black that indicated the presence of the disease.

"Yer clear," she reassured her companions. "The beast is just a beast after all."

With sighs of relief, the crew began to recover, cleaning off their weapons

CHAPTER 13

and helping each other to their feet. Fankin and Paddy tended to Kurt's injured leg, while Leeta and Odo headed back to the entrance to get some fresh air after their ordeal. But as they approached the entryway, they heard quiet voices muttering in an unknown language. Leeta paused and leaned over to Odo.

"I don't like the sound of that...we'd better warn the others, she whispered.

Odo nodded slightly. "Sounds vaguely Elven, but...*older*, and—I don't know how to explain it, but—*darker*, somehow. I can't make out the words, but the tone sounds sinister."

They turned and headed stealthily back to the room from which they'd come. When they got back, Kryda was sitting on the cold floor sipping idly from her wineskin, while Fankin and Paddy continued to fuss over Kurt. Everyone looked up as Leeta rounded the corner with Odo close on her heels.

"We heard some voices back near the entrance," she explained. "Didn't sound friendly. I have a feeling it won't be as easy to leave this place as it was to get in."

Kryda stood up, her interest piqued.

"Why don't we go git 'em, then?" she suggested. "More fun than sittin' around here."

She stood up and sauntered out of the room, without even checking to see if the others were following. The rest of the crew looked askance at Odo, expecting him to insist on formulating some kind of plan first, but he just shrugged and headed after Kryda. Grinning and shaking their heads, the rest of the crew followed along.

Odo caught up with Kryda and took the lead to check for traps, and Paddy stayed close behind, since he could speak Elven, but thought it best to keep the well-armoured dwarf between himself and the unfamiliar elves. As the crew approached the entrance, they were met with silence. After a moment, Paddy called out in Elven, his tone commanding.

"We know you are here. Show yourselves!"

Odo turned and whispered something to Fankin, who nodded and twirled his fingers. As he did so, an eerie wail echoed around them, and Kryda started nervously, readying her pickaxe. Leeta grinned and nudged her.

"Psst! It's alright, Kryda. Fankin is making that sound."

"I knew tha'," Kryda muttered. She lowered her pickaxe, but remained vigilant.

As the echoing wail died away, the crew heard light, ethereal voices giggling slightly in response. Fankin perked his long ears, searching for the source of the sound, and pointed silently towards the eastern wall of the entryway. Murmuring a spell, Fankin flicked his fingers one by one, releasing a small ball of light with each movement. The lights danced along the wall, illuminating the corridor. The crew peered across the room, but still couldn't make anything out. Kurt and Kryda stepped forward, hesitantly—but they weren't silent enough. An arrow zipped past Kryda's head, thudding into the wall directly beside her.

Kryda whirled around, pointing her pickaxe accusingly in the general direction of her assailant. "HA! I knew ye were hidin' up there! Ye cannae stay hidden from us. We'll be findin' ye!"

Fankin's dancing lights bobbed up in the direction she was pointing, illuminating the two elves, who were positioned above the group on the catwalk that arched over the eastern wall. The archer in front, holding his bow lightly at the ready, stepped forward with a smile and nocked another arrow.

"Surely you did not believe that we were hiding from you. If we had indeed been hiding, you never would have known we were here at all. On the contrary; we were merely having a bit of sport with you before sending you on your way."

The ranger nodded gracefully to Kryda, his smile widening, but his eyes hardened. "Whether you depart dead or alive is yet to be seen, my dear dwarf. That shot was simply a warning. If you insist on continuing whatever it is you came here to do, then I shan't miss the next one."

"Let's just take out the catwalk and leave them in the rubble, eh?" Odo muttered to Fankin. The elf ranger whirled upon Odo and fired a shot that wouldn't have missed if the rogue hadn't brought his arm up quickly, the arrow embedding itself in his bracer. The archer stepped back, baring his

CHAPTER 13

teeth in a hiss, as the second elf began to conjure a spell.

"Watch out for that mage!" Leeta warned the group. Odo flung a dagger at the elf in an attempt to disrupt her cast, but he was too late. The dagger sliced across her arm, but she had already released her fireball. It spiralled into Odo's shoulder, setting his cloak aflame. He discarded it, cursing, as she let out a high-pitched laugh.

"Now we're even, halfling!" she preened, but her triumph was cut short when a stone from Leeta's sling zipped into the wall behind her head.

"Damn those flaming balls of magic!" Odo howled as Fankin flung his own fireball at the elven archer, singeing his long hair.

"Curse you, gnome!" the ranger spat at Fankin, preparing to nock another arrow.

Throughout this altercation, Kurt had decided to take Odo's initial advice. He seized Leeta's torch and began setting the pillars of the catwalk on fire. After dropping the torch next to the pillar that was closest to the elves, he and Leeta headed for the ladder on the other side of the catwalk in an attempt to flank them.

Fankin scrambled up the ladder of the western catwalk across from the hostile elves, attempting to better position himself for further ranged attacks. The ranger prepared to fire another arrow at the gnome, but Odo flung his second dagger at the ranger to try and keep the elves' attention on the lower level while his teammates got into position. He was aiming for the ranger's chest, but the elf spotted the dagger and leaped aside at the last second with a hiss, taking it in his shoulder instead.

"Ha! That'll slow him down, at least!" Odo muttered gleefully to himself. The elven mage, on the other hand, had turned her attentions toward the ladder, where Kurt had just crested the top. She launched another fireball, and Kurt leaned quickly to one side, but it singed his ear.

Kryda, noticing that neither elf was paying attention to her, motioned to Paddy, who quickly sensed her meaning. Taking her hand, he murmured a swift blessing, granting Kryda protection against the flames that now licked hungrily up the beams supporting the catwalk. Kryda nodded her thanks and headed towards the pillars.

As Kurt clambered up onto the catwalk and began to charge the ranger, the elf turned on him, but the paladin raised his shield and deflected it. Leeta, following close behind Kurt, scrambled up and around him, headed for the mage.

Fankin took advantage of the elves' distraction and edged closer to the catwalk, preparing for a more close-range attack. Meanwhile, Odo fired his crossbow at the mage, but missed badly, nearly hitting Leeta, who was closing in on her.

Meanwhile, the fire Kurt had set beneath the catwalk had begun to take hold. Kryda, taking advantage of this, struck out with her pickaxe and attacked the supporting beam beneath the mage, who had retreated in an attempt to heal herself. The catwalk snapped and began to crumble, and the elf lost her footing and tumbled to an abrupt end as her body slammed into the stone floor.

However, Kryda's triumph was quickly followed by dismay as the catwalk continued to collapse towards both the ranger elf and her teammates. As the catwalk fell away beneath him, the ranger caught hold of a rail with his left hand, but his wounded right arm failed him, and he dropped his bow. Leeta was nearly caught in the collapsing catwalk as well, but Kurt reached out and caught her arm, hauling her back to her feet.

Seeing his opportunity, Fankin lobbed a fireball at the ranger, who was clinging desperately to the railing. His shot found its mark, and the archer lost his grip, falling to the same fate as his partner. Kurt and Leeta, however, managed to make their way back down the ladder before the entire catwalk fell, and they fled to the far side of the room with Kryda close behind. Just as they emerged from beneath it, the rest of the eastern catwalk collapsed to the floor, flaming beams raining down around them.

Fankin leaped down from the western catwalk as the flames began to spread towards his perch and followed close behind the rest of the crew as they hastily evacuated the entryway, stumbling back out into the sunlight as the smoke from their battleground billowed out around them.

CHAPTER 13

* * *

As the crew stood just outside the entrance to the sewer, stunned and trying to catch their breath, Kryda passed around her wineskin for everyone to have a stiff drink. "We'll be needin' to get back to the city for some more o' tha' after this," she said dryly.

Paddy was the first to respond, leaning on his staff as he nodded gracefully to Kryda. "I agree, but first we must notify the Governor of these elves. I expect they are not the only ones in the city; I saw a mark on the arm of the ranger when he first drew his bow. It was the brand of an outlaw. To endure the stench of this place simply in order to remain hidden—I am certain their presence indicates much more misfortune to come."

The crew remained silent for a moment, glancing at each other with concern in their eyes. Leeta spoke up next.

"We should bring the skull of the beast back with us, too. I don't think that was a chance encounter, either—it seemed like it was guarding the area."

Despite their reluctance to re-enter the sewers, the crew gathered the evidence they needed to present to the Governor, as well as to study for any more clues they might have missed. Just as they were about to exit the sewers once again, Odo reached out a hand to stop them.

"Did anyone else hear that?"

"Ach, wha' *now?*" groaned Kryda, but everyone else shushed her. There was silence for a moment, but just as Kryda was about to speak up again, the group heard a soft moan coming from the hallway on the opposite side of the entryway where they had encountered the elves.

"Sounds just like your mother did last night, Kurt," Fankin whispered to the paladin, who shot him a stern look.

"Don't be a dick, Fankin!" Leeta smacked Fankin in the back of the head with something rather soft—he hoped it was not yet another disembodied limb. "Don't you think we should check it out?" she hissed, stepping between Kurt and Fankin, who were still glaring daggers at each other.

"It could be a trap," Odo warned her.

"But what if someone needs help?" Kurt broke in, shooting one last warning glance at Fankin before turning back toward his companions. "We should at least have a look."

"What do you think, Kryda?" Leeta asked.

"Aye, I'm fine with tha'." Kryda replied casually, seizing Fankin's collar as he made faces at Kurt and hauling him back toward the rest of the adventurers. "What d'ye say, Fankin?"

His fun spoiled, Fankin readjusted his clothing and armour, sulking. "Of course I'm coming," he grumbled, rolling his eyes. "You lot are no fun sometimes, you know that?"

"I'll be plenty o' fun after we be findin' some fresh brew," Kryda promised him. "Come on, let's get this done with first."

The three of them headed back down the corridor until they came upon a room alight with torches, a large pit full of water rippling in the center.

"How deep do ya think tha' be?" Kryda wondered aloud.

"Don't know, don't care. It smells horrid! I'm not going to try to find out. There's room enough to go around." Leeta took the lead and stepped onto the ledge surrounding the water, hoping that it didn't give way and that she didn't slip. She could swim well enough, even in her gear, but she certainly didn't want to touch whatever was in there.

It was darker up ahead, and the moaning grew louder as the adventurers made their way around the well. When they finally reached the other side, they saw nothing but a short corridor ahead, which didn't seem to have any other hallways or doors branching off of it.

Waving her friends to follow her, Leeta stepped into the corridor, with Kryda close upon her heels. Fankin wasn't far behind, but luckily for him, it was far enough that he avoided following them directly into the pit trap that gave way beneath their feet. He reached his arms back toward Paddy and Odo to warn them to stop.

After taking a moment to laugh at the two women as they coughed and brushed dust and rubble from their clothes, Fankin took the rope that Odo handed him and lowered it into the pit so they could climb out. When they had safely ascended, Kryda punched Fankin's arm so hard that he almost fell

CHAPTER 13

in as well.

Fankin snorted, rubbing his sore arm and glaring at Kryda. "I got you out, didn't I? And how are we going to get across now?"

"Piece o' honey-cake," Kryda replied airily, taking the rope from Fankin and tying it around the handle of her pickaxe. Swinging it in a circle, as widely as she could in the enclosed space, she launched it toward the ceiling above the pit. It embedded itself deep into the ceiling, sprinkling more rubble into the pit.

Wrapping the other end of the rope around her arm, Kryda gave it a couple of hefty tugs, before grinning at her comrades and jumping off the side of the pit. She swung in a wide arc, pulling herself slightly higher on the rope just before reaching the other side of the pit, where she released her grip on the rope and leapt to the other side, rolling on her shoulder to break the momentum.

She looked back at her friends, expecting them to be impressed, but Odo was already gesturing for her to throw the rope back across so he could swing himself across as well. Leeta and Paddy merely looked amused by her little stunt, and Fankin stared at her in complete terror for a brief moment before schooling his features into a look of utter indifference. Kryda tossed the end of the rope back to their side with a sullen look and waited for the others to cross.

"Shortest goes first," Leeta smirked, bowing slightly as she presented the rope to Fankin, who shot her an irritable look. Once all four of them had made it to the other side of the pit, they peered carefully around the corner and found themselves staring into an open room.

Kryda was the first to step into the room, and she felt a tingling as she did, so followed by such an overpowering stench that forced even her hardy dwarven stomach to empty itself. The rest of the crew stopped short, and Leeta reached out her hand to touch Kryda's shoulder, but stopped as she felt the tingling of the force field as well. Still retching, Kryda got to her feet and backed out of the room, motioning the others to stay back.

"I'm alright," she gasped. "Tha' was *foul*, though!" She spat on the floor, trying to clear her tongue of the horrid taste.

Odo stepped forward, staring past the force field, then turned slowly back to the crew.

"You all might want to look at this," he told them grimly.

They peered inside the room and noticed for the first time that the floor was entirely obscured by bones in varying states of decay.

"I suppose it's too much to ask that those bones stay dead...?" Fankin gulped, his voice trembling. Unfortunately, he was right. The crew began backing away slowly as the bones rattled, then began to reassemble themselves, just like the first skeleton they'd found. They all realized at the same time that there was no way they could face an army of that size without much more preparation, and after a series of quick, terrified glances at each other for reassurance that wasn't there, they turned tail and fled.

As they ran frantically back towards the entrance, Kryda pausing only to yank her pickaxe from the ceiling, they heard the moaning again, echoing through the corridors. It no longer sounded anything like a person in need of help, but rather something deeper and more sinister. Spurred on as the sound grew louder, the adventurers burst out of the entrance to the sewer and stared at each other with wide, terrified eyes.

"There's no way we can fight that many," Kurt coughed, hunched over, hands on his knees as he gasped for breath.

"We must report all of this Harden at once." Paddy added, and the rest of the crew nodded in agreement. After a brief rest, they decided that they'd better head back to town to have their wounds treated, restock their supplies, and come up with some sort of plan to face the literal army of skeletons before returning to the sewers. They would also have a little chat with the Governor regarding their current payment; they all agreed that their first mission was turning out to be a lot harder than it was supposed to have been.

CHAPTER 13

14

Chapter 14

The Retreat

The crew were all quiet during the walk back to the city, including Kryda, whose wineskin was bone dry. At the gates, Paddy sent a guard to Harden with a brief description of their day.. Their first stop, of course, was the healer's cabin. They'd all suffered some injury or another, and they knew that even a scrape could be deadly in the fight to come.

After their wounds had been treated, their next stop was the Governor's manor—or it would have been, if Kryda hadn't insisted on refilling her wineskin on the way. Unfortunately, the Governor was not in when they stopped by, so they left him a note—along with the trophies from their excursion. They knew with a grim certainty that he would send for them as soon as he read their message.

While they waited, they split up to gather whatever weapons and equipment each would need for what they were preparing to face the next day, hoping that whatever they'd awoken in the sewers would stay there until

CHAPTER 14

they could go back and deal with it.

When they'd finished replenishing their supplies, they all met back at the tavern to come up with a new plan of attack. Fankin was the last to arrive, but the first to launch into a story, as usual.

"So, I walk into the magic shop, right? And there's this woman behind the counter with absolutely *massive* knockers. Other than that, she wasn't much to look at, so I figured I might have some luck if I poured on the charm." Kurt, who had come in just before Fankin, rolled his eyes with a grin and tipped back his glass. Fankin shot him a glare, then continued.

"So, I say to her, 'Let me have a look at your wares,' and I wink at her. And you know what she says to me? She says to me, with a seriously poor attempt at being sultry, she says, 'They're double D's,' and she winks right back at me. So now I'm thinking I've got a real shot at a good deal. I see this ring with a feather on it and I ask her, 'How much for this beauty from the beautiful lady?' And she completely stonefaces me! She looks me right in the eyes and just deadpans like: '5000 gold!' I was *crushed*, I tell you!" Fankin feigned offence in such a dramatic manner that Kryda almost lost some of her ale through her nose.

"So I played it cool, like, 'I'm sure you mean well, and would never knowingly overcharge a simple gnome such as myself, but you see, I know a little something about this kind of work, and I don't think it's as valuable as you've been lead to believe. However, I am willing to offer a very generous price for this piece, despite my concerns about its worth. How about 1500 gold pieces?' Now, I have to admit, she handled herself pretty well here. She only looked offended for a split second at my lowball offer before smoothing her features over and bringing on the *honey!*" Fankin shouted, banging his mug of ale down on the table as the liquid sloshed over his hand.

"'Oh, you must be mistaken, sir!' she says in this real high voice, batting her eyelashes at me, 'I would be a fool to not know how to price the items in my very own shop! I can assure you, I do know how much something like this is worth!' Well, by now she knew that she had me, and she flashed me a great big grin. But then she says to me, 'You are rather charming, though,' and she leans in *close*. 'Maybe, just for you, I could make a special little deal.' And she taps her pudgy fingers on her chin a few times, like she's deep in thought, and then she says, 'I think I would sell it to *you* for only 3500 gold, sir,' and she put her hand close enough to mine that she could tap at my finger." Fankin leaned forward and demonstrated on Kryda, gently drumming his fingers on the back of her hand.

"I says to her, 'I meant no disrespect, ma'am, and I am certainly inclined to trust your judgment on such things, of course. You may have heard, though, that my friends and I—we're on a very special mission, to clean up some… problems that the city has been having. You know, with the sewage. The Governor would be *ever* so grateful if you could aid us in our quest. With that in mind, I can offer you 2000 gold for this ring.' Well, let me tell you, when I said that, she *yanked* her hand away like I'd burned her, but she says to me, 'In light of the work you are doing for the good of the city, I suppose I could go just a little lower. But 3000 gold is absolutely the best I can do for you without going out of business, and let's face it: without my shop, this city would have a lot more problems than just some stinky sewers.' And then she wrinkles her nose, just like this!" Fankin pulled his hand away from Kryda's and pointed to his own nose, scrunching it up as much as he possibly could and affecting a very convincing air of disgust

"I thought to myself, *you have no idea, lady!* But I just smiled and told her it was still too much. Well, long story short, we dropped the act after that, and I ended up with these." He held out some scrolls and vials for the others to see, but Paddy was the only one who could read the labels on the scrolls well enough to understand what Fankin was even talking about.

"Roughly translated, these are fiery palms, burning arrow and healing elixir. Fankin, you already know all of these spells."

"Well, yes, but I can only cast a few per day, so this way I have some extra just in case. Besides, if someone else needs something other than a physical weapon, I can share." He indicated Kryda, but smacked her hand away when she reached eagerly for the one that would shoot fire.

"*Only* if it's an emergency!" he told her sharply, shoving the parchments hastily back into his pack. "What about all of you? Anything to share?" He looked over at Odo, who was sitting contemplatively across the table from

CHAPTER 14

him. "Odo? Where'd you get off to?"

"I was cloaked in darkness, stalking my prey..." Odo began somberly, pulling the hood of his cloak over his face, then sat back with a grin and a wave of his hand. "Nah, I just popped on over to the rogue shrine and made an offering for luck. Not that *I* need it, but I figured it couldn't hurt for *some* of us—" he looked pointedly at Kryda, "—to be blessed with a little more stealth and caution." Kryda made a dramatic show of being deeply offended, which made everyone laugh.

"Dare I ask what were you doing while we were out, Kryda?" Paddy inquired.

"Yer lookin' at it. Best way for a dwarf to heal up is to drink as much as possible of the best ale they c'n find!" Kryda peered into her stein. "Now tha' ye mention it, I think I'm still hurtin..." That drew another chuckle out of the crew as well, but Kryda continued. "Then there was tha' kender over there, who tried to get me out of me armour...but seriously, who'd 'e think would be takin' charge in that scenario, am I right? I also did nae wish to come out of there missing anythin' important." She patted her coin purse for show, but then ran her fingers lightly along the engraving on her pickaxe when the laughter died down and everyone's attention was drawn away to Kurt, who spoke up next.

"Leeta and I had some fun with the lads at the barracks. Remember how they were giving us a hard time the other day? Saying this quest wasn't fit for someone from the Academy, and that we only passed so the Optio could get us out of there, and whatnot? Well, we showed them the beast's head, and let me tell you, they changed their tune soon enough!" Leeta and Kurt were nodding at each other in satisfaction through the whole story until Fankin smacked Kurt in the arm.

"We left that there for the Governor, so we have proof that this quest is much harder than it was supposed to be! You know, so we can get a better payout!? Where is it now?"

Before Kurt could open his mouth to reply, Leeta jumped in.

"We put it back, of course. Besides, it paid off—some of the older, wiser adventurers were impressed enough that they offered us some tips on how to deal with those skeletons we left in the sewers. Most of it was only useful for my skillset, but there were some tips regarding nature magic as well. They said fire is good, too, if we have any casters." She nodded to Paddy and Fankin.

"That's perfect." Fankin sat back in his chair, gratified, and Paddy nodded his acknowledgement. "What about you, Paddy?" Fankin prodded him. "Over at the Academy practicing again?"

Paddy smiled ruefully. "If you can call it practice, I suppose. My magic was quite spent, so I spent my time studying some wonderful old tomes, and discovered a few new incantations and prayers that may come in handy."

As Paddy was speaking, the barmaid came over to refill everyone's drinks, and the kender Kryda had mentioned earlier was following close behind her. He hassled the barmaid to hurry back to his table, before turning to flirt with Kryda once again.

"You should seriously consider coming over to my table and leaving these poor sods to their own devices for the night." He winked at Kryda, grabbing the barmaid's arm as she started to walk away. "Maybe we can steal this one to join us as well!" he leered, tilting his head up to stare at the woman's breasts. Kryda grabbed him by the collar and yanked him backwards.

"Sod off, half pint!" she spat, then tossed him onto the floor as if he weighed no more than a kitten. She turned to apologize to the barmaid. "I'm sorry. Ye shouldn't have to deal with the likes of 'im."

"Oh, don't worry," the barmaid replied, as they watched the kender brush himself off and stumble away. "He won't be a bother much longer. I have a special drink coming for *him!*" She smiled conspiratorially at Kryda, then skipped away with a devilish grin on her face. Kryda sat back down and winked at her companions.

"I like that one. A bit scary, though," she remarked, slamming back her ale. The others raised their glasses to that and quickly followed suit.

* * *

CHAPTER 14

As they had expected, the crew were awoken the next morning by a summons from the Governor, who wanted to speak with them to clarify exactly what they had discovered in the city's sewers. Harden met them at the Governor's manor with an apology for not meeting them the previous evening and looking extremely concerned when the crew expanded on their experience in the sewers as well as Gibbs' concerns.

"It would likely be best if I came along with you when you return," Harden told them. "For now, let's just see what the Governor has to say about this."

They were escorted into the Governor's office, where he welcomed them warmly, but they could hear the worry tightening his voice. He told them that he was loath to offer them higher pay, but he did agree to provide them with compensation for the extra equipment and items that they had purchased to help complete the job. He also offered to pay for their food and lodgings thus far, as well as for as long as they would need in order to finish their mission. The adventurers were disappointed that they wouldn't be making any extra gold, but they were very happy to hear that they wouldn't be paying out of pocket for their expenses, either. The Governor immediately sent out notices to the tavern, the Academy and relevant shops that they were to forward all the adventurers' further bills to the Governor himself.

"The city will be abuzz about this, of course," he told them, "but I do *not* want to cause a panic, so please keep these details discreet." The crew glanced around at each other cautiously, knowing that whispers would be coming from the barracks already. "Keep me informed if you run into any further problems. We need to have this…infection dealt with, before the people of the city find out and cause a riot. I wouldn't be surprised if the recent mysterious deaths might possibly have had something to do with this as well," he said, grimly, stroking his perfectly shaven chin.

"What deaths? You didn't mention that any suspicious deaths were involved," Leeta glowered.

"Yes, that might have been pertinent information for us to have," Paddy agreed.

The Governor sighed. "Well, it didn't occur to me that they might be connected at all until now. The city's healers have all failed to find the cause of these deaths, but perhaps you should speak to them before you return to the sewers, just to ascertain whether or not they may have any further information for you." He pulled out a map of the city and plucked his quill pen from its ink pot, then carefully marked the various locations of the city's healers on the map. There was one in each direction—north, east, west, and south—with each evenly spaced location distanced exactly two thirds of the way from the center of the city.

Odo picked up the map and studied it. "We should split up, and meet back at the tavern after we've spoken to them."

"I'll take the east," Fankin offered.

"Ye think we're all daft, do ye?" Kryda snorted. "The tavern's in the east, thickhead, so you'd be having the shortest trip, then, wouldn't ye?" She gave him a playful shove.

"That's enough, you two," Harden intervened.

The Governor nodded gratefully at Harden. "Ada is the elder healer, and therefore the most likely to be your best source of information. She is in the east, so you should go there first. She will be able to tell you if any of the others are worth venturing to, but if any of them have information of particular importance, it will almost certainly be her."

"We will *all* go," Harden announced, glaring meaningfully at his crew to warn them not to protest. "Thank you, Governor, for your help."

* * *

The healer's door opened abruptly just as Harden raised his hand to knock. "Come in, come in," she said impatiently, beckoning to the adventurers, a knowing smile on her weary face. "I thought you might be coming to find me soon enough."

Harden stepped forward to greet her, but she raised one finger in protest. "No need for pleasant small talk, Captain. I sense you young ones have an important story to tell me. I'd like you to tell it, and when you've finished,

CHAPTER 14

I'll have a story of my own to give you in return." She poured them each a glass of wine, then one for herself, and finally plopped down decisively on a chair and waited.

After glancing at Harden for approval, Kryda opened her mouth to speak. She meant to begin with their experience in the sewer, but for some strange reason, she felt compelled to tell the healer everything, beginning with the story of her encounter with the diseased boar.

As Kryda talked, she felt more and more as if she were losing control of her own tale, as if it were spilling out of her mouth like wine from a burst wineskin. She told the healer of the way she'd seen the sickness grow stronger in response to fear or anger, as well as the healing song she'd sung both to the boar and then with the little girl in the village.

Kryda's companions stared at her open-mouthed, having only previously heard part of the story. The healer listened intently to Kryda, nodding here and there and urging Kryda to go on whenever she hesitated. By the time Kryda had finished, Ada sat silent for a moment, tapping her glass of wine with her fingers. Then, she nodded once again, more slowly this time.

"Yes, I knew this day would come," she murmured, half to herself. "I cannot tell you everything you desire to know, but I can give you something that will help you. First, though, a story." Harden began to protest that their mission was urgent, but she once again wagged her finger at him. "I know what you are trying to say, Captain, but I promise you that this is a tale that will do you good to hear. Now, let me begin." She leaned forward on her chair and looked each of the adventurers in the eyes in turn. Then, she took a deep breath and spoke.

"Long ago, four sisters lived outside this city, before it became a city and was yet a growing village. They were the four daughters of the village leader, who lived in a great house at the center of the village with their mother, who was the elder healer. One day, the four sisters were each in their own homes, preparing meals for a feast that was to be held in the house of their father. But they all felt deep in their hearts that something was terribly wrong. They felt compelled to return to the village, and when they did so, they saw their father's house in flames. The village was paralyzed by panic, but the sisters pushed through the crowd into the center of the village. They could hardly see each other through the smoke, but as if in a trance, they reached up as one, touching their fingers together. A blue light emanated from the tips of their fingers, and they looked up to the sky as the heavens opened and rain poured down from the clouds. The rain put out the fire, and the village rejoiced." The healer paused, smiling slightly.

"Of course, it is remembered now that the men of the village brought water from the river, and the story of the sisters became a legend that few still believe. But the story is true. After the death of their parents, the sisters, who had studied both the art of magic and all manner of healing with their mother, became the village's new healers. As the village grew and prospered, the Four Healers remained, passing on their healing gifts and their magic to their descendants. Their daughters would inherit their homes when they passed on, and the city built up around them. And so it has always been—until now."

"Until now?" Paddy asked. "What has changed?"

The healer gazed at him sadly. "As you know by now, I and my fellow healers are the descendants of the four sisters, but we will be the last. We are, all of us, barren."

"I'm sorry," Harden murmured. "But—Ada—"

The healer interrupted him for the third time, much to the amusement of his crew. "Yes, I know. You wish to know what this story means for your mission. I cannot tell you, but know this: darkness is stirring, as you have already seen, and ancient evils are returning. The veil is lifting, Captain. This is only the beginning. And that is why I know what I must do." The healer stood and rummaged around in one of her cupboards as the adventurers glanced anxiously at one another, puzzled by her cryptic warning.

Ada turned back to the group, clutching something tightly in one hand. She beckoned to Kryda. "Come here, child. Kryda, isn't it?"

Kryda nodded dumbly, looking curiously into the healer's blue eyes. Ada opened her hand to reveal a small, bright blue gem resting in her palm, and rested her other hand gently on Kryda's shoulder.

"This is what I would have passed on to my daughter," she sighed, gazing sadly down at the gem. "But the gods clearly meant for the line of my family

CHAPTER 14

to end here. That is why I am certain that I am to gift the magic of my ancestors to one destined to fight against the coming darkness. Take this," she continued, pressing the gem into Kryda's hand. "You will find it helpful. It has great power to heal, but it cannot be used to hurt—though, you do not seem like one who would need such a warning," she said, smiling understandingly at Kryda. "Use it well, and use it sparingly."

Chapter 15

The Return

The crew were somber as they departed the healer's hut, and the reality of the unpleasantness that awaited them in the immediate future really began to sink in as they got farther and farther away from the comfortable familiarity of the city. Their feet dragged as they plodded glumly back toward the sewers, with the notable exception of Harden, who remained alert and guarded.

"Tell me again about the room at the end of the sewers," he ordered them. "I want us to be as prepared as possible."

"It was horrible," Leeta groaned. "I could see it clearly enough, but I only got the smell as I pulled Kryda back away from the room when she was done retching."

Harden glanced at Kryda. "Must have been a pretty nasty room, to have had such an effect on even a dwarven stomach."

"That i' was," she replied with a grimace, gagging. "There's some kind o' barrier—magical in nature, by all likelihood—tha's keepin' in the worst o'

CHAPTER 15

the stink."

"If even a magical barrier is not enough to contain the stench—" Harden began, but he was interrupted by the sound of Odo retching as he emptied the contents of his stomach, and they were still quite a distance from the entrance to the sewer.

The group stopped and fell silent, staring at the halfling as he straightened back up and wiped off his mouth. "Just had too much to eat at the tavern," he joked weakly, but he was deathly pale, and his mouth was drawn.

The rest of the group felt their own stomachs lurch as the scent wafting from the entrance rolled over them as well. They stared at it in horror; it had not smelled nearly this awful yesterday.

"I say we leave *that* room for last today," Kurt suggested grimly. "Maybe we'll find something elsewhere that'll give us a better idea of what we're up against in there." He looked askance at Harden, who paused for a moment, before nodding in agreement. With barely concealed sighs of relief, the group continued onward.

They were grateful when they entered the sewer and the smell did not actually seem to worsen immediately. Kurt and Kryda led the way, as was fitting for the members of the party who relied most on brute strength and wore the heaviest armour, but they weren't always the ones with the keenest senses. When they saw no immediate threat, they motioned for the others to come forward.

"Kin ye use some magic fer seein' if there be...well, other magic? Er, anythin' threatenin' at all?" Kryda asked, shuffling her feet awkwardly. Fankin and Paddy stepped forward, followed closely by a curious Leeta, but as they entered the room, all the torches that had been burning low on the wall sconces snuffed out—they didn't need to use their own magic to know that there was magic afoot.

It took a moment for Kryda's eyes to adjust to the darkness, but as they did, she saw that the floor was undulating. "Snakes!" she cried, but it was too late. One of them was already striking at Leeta's leg. Fortunately, her armour was thick enough to stop the venomous fangs from piercing her skin, but it quickly wound itself around her leg and began constricting. Odo was very

153

nearly bitten as well, but he managed to roll backward out of the mass of assailants in response to Kryda's warning.

"Bollocks! Fankin, kin ye nae do a thing about these buggers? Try an' talk to 'em, dammit!" Kryda shouted. Fankin stepped back behind Odo for protection and began hissing thickly through his teeth. To everyone's relief, the snakes began to slowly back away, and the one clinging tightly to Leeta's leg dropped back to the floor. They still seemed very territorial, though, especially when Odo veered off the main path to re-light the torches as the adventurers passed through.

As the crew entered the next room, it appeared to be empty but for a small dias topped with an hourglass. Kurt approached the dais and lifted the hourglass carefully, squinting at the inscription on the bottom as he read it aloud.

"I prepared explo—" he began, but was quickly interrupted by Fankin, who snatched the artifact from his hands with a cry.

"You shouldn't have touched this, Kurt! We have to go! NOW!" Fankin replaced the hourglass upside down so the sands began to run and led the crew to the next room as quickly as possible. Odo stopped near the door and knelt to inspect it.

"Let me check—" he began, but once again Fankin interrupted, shoving him unceremoniously through the doorway.

"No time! That *was* the trap!" Fankin shouted, continuing to rush the crew through the door. Odo looked very relieved as they crossed the threshold with no incident. Once they were all safely through the entrance, Fankin slammed the door behind them, yelling over their questions and protests for them to help him brace the door. They were still arguing when an explosion rocked the floor, throwing them off their footing and knocking Odo and Fankin, the smallest members of the party, completely to the ground

"What the hell was that??" gasped Leeta. Fankin directed his answer to Kurt.

"There was a fancy 'V' inscribed on that podium," he explained, still trying to catch his breath. "I couldn't remember why it looked familiar until you started reading the inscription. 'V'—no one remembers the full name, he's

CHAPTER 15

just called V—was a famous and powerful wizard who was notorious for his little explosive traps. You pick it up to read the inscription, and just before you've finished, it goes off in your hand. Luckily for us, this one was linked to the hourglass as a timer."

"Then why not just put the hourglass back down the right way up?" Odo asked.

"Because I assumed that would mean 'zero' and trigger the explosion right away. I took the chance that the sands would at least last long enough for us to get out of there."

"Good thinking, Fankin," Harden praised him.

As they talked, Leeta waved her torch around the room, wary of threats lurking in dark corners after their experience with the creature from last time. But the room held nothing but a table, which she promptly flipped in frustration at the lack of both information and treasure.

After Leeta duly relayed her lack of findings to the crew, they left the room, passing into a long empty corridor. By the time they finally reached the main eastern chamber of the sewers, which was marked by neither a change in decor or a door, they had grown rather complacent with boredom.

Their carelessness led them directly into a small pack of goblins. A javelin buried itself in Kryda's arm as she crossed the threshold. Fankin instinctively summoned his fireball, but completely missed the goblins and instead lit a tapestry on fire. The resulting smoke made it even more difficult to see what was in the room ahead, but the cackles of the goblins were unmistakable.

Kryda edged around the corner, peering through the smoke with eyes watering in the direction of the javelin stab she'd received. She could just barely make out the goblin that had attacked her not far away. It seemed to be looking more at the gnome with the flaming hands than at her, so she took a page from Odo's book and advanced silently in the darkest shadows along the wall, preparing to attack.

Leeta entered the room slowly at first, but as soon as she broke through the cloud of smoke and could make out her targets, she charged in and slew one almost immediately. The goblins clearly weren't expecting such an aggressive tactic, and the rest of the crew took this as their cue to take action. Fankin lobbed another fireball at the goblin right next to Leeta and stopped its attack dead. Because that's what it was—dead.

As the rest of the crew charged in, Odo spotted a pillar to the one side of the cluster of goblins and grinned to himself. *Dumb things, staying close together like that*, he thought gleefully to himself, and crept along the walls until he reached the pillar, concealing himself behind it and settling into the perfect flanking position for anyone who preferred to sneak up on his enemies.

The goblin that Kryda was stalking must have heard her approach, because he looked away from the flaming gnome and sniffed the air, searching for her. Unfortunately for him, she was much closer than he'd anticipated, and after throwing his javelin, he was left unarmed. She leapt at him, closing the distance, and knocked him in the head with the blunt side of her pickaxe. He crumpled soundlessly to the floor, without even a drop of blood. *No point in makin' a mess just for a little goblin*, Kryda thought to herself.

She checked quickly to make sure that he was indeed dead, then headed toward the remaining goblins to help finish them off, noticing that one was preparing to lob another javelin, this time at Leeta. She didn't make it in time to stop the goblin from hurling his javelin, which buried itself deep into Leeta's thigh, but she did immediately bowl him over so Leeta could get in the final swing and exact her revenge on the foul little creature.

Fankin spotted one more of the buggers sneaking around the furthest pillar. He picked up the javelin that the first goblin had dropped near the entryway and flung it across the room with a yell. The javelin only grazed the back of the goblin's leg as he disappeared behind the pillar. Almost immediately there was a yelp, then silence. Everyone held their breath, waiting for the creature to peek back around, but the tiny figure that emerged was not a goblin. Odo stepped out from the behind the pillar, casually wiping off his blades. They all relaxed noticeably at his sly little grin and shrug.

"Is tha' the last of 'em?" Kryda asked, trying to catch her breath. The others all looked instinctively around the room for any survivors, and began to re-light the torches as the smoke cleared. When they were convinced there were no longer any remaining threats—or anything of value—they searched for any passageways that would lead them on from there. Kryda in particular seemed extremely eager to leave.

"We need to be gettin' out o' here. This room smells almost as bad as tha' other one," she groaned, the mere memory making her stomach turn.

Just as the adventurers began to think that the room was a dead end, Odo found an opening. He called the crew over. "What do we think of this?"

Leeta bent over to look into the tiny space, gagging from the stench that emanated from it.

"We're not going through there." She turned and looked back at Harden, who seemed to be deep in thought. "Are we?" she asked, half-pleading.

"Wait a moment," Fankin called. The adventurers turned to look at the gnome, who was staring intently at a piece of parchment, counting under his breath as he hastily sketched something on the scroll. Leeta hoped desperately that whatever Fankin was fiddling with would give them another option.

"What 'ave ye there, Fankin?" Kryda inquired, sidling up beside him and standing on her toes to get a peek. "Yu've made a map, ye brilliant bugger?" she cried, clapping a hand down on his shoulder. "Tell me it's not sayin' we gotta go thru tha', though!"

Fankin did not look pleased by Kryda's antics, but he did look pleased with the result of his map. Everyone stared at the gnome, waiting patiently for his answer.

"The good news is that we don't have to go through there, but the bad news is that we're still going to have to endure that smell. This tunnel appears to lead directly back into that warded room."

Harden looked pensive as he took at look at the map for himself.

"What're ye thinkin' there, Cap'n?" Kryda asked.

Harden studied the map intently. "That means this doorway here—" he pointed at the map, looking to Fankin for confirmation—"is where you encountered the warding. So...if you couldn't smell it on the outside when you were there, why can we smell it so clearly coming from this side?" He smiled knowingly at Fankin, a grin which was quickly returned by the gnome as the Captain's meaning sank in. Leeta and Kryda looked askance at each other, but neither seemed to be in on whatever secret Harden and Fankin had stumbled upon. Harden nodded permission to the gnome, still smiling. "Do it."

Fankin approached the passage holding a cloth over his nose. "PRES-TI-DI-GI-TA-TION!" he shouted at the top of his lungs, the muffled word echoing through the passage. Standing up and brushing himself off with an air of satisfaction, he removed the cloth from his nose.

Harden chuckled. "If there was anything in there to hear that, it should at least distract them. Let's head back to the main entrance." He handed the map back to Fankin, who returned it to his satchel, and led the way as the group headed back out of the sewers.

* * *

When they finally emerged back into the sunlight, they gulped deep breaths of fresh air. Their stomachs had just begun to settle when none other than old man Gibbs burst into the clearing by the entryway.

"I'm glad I found you out here!" he cried delightedly. "How is it going in there? What did you find?" The old man listened intently Kryda filled him in, looking increasingly serious and concerned as she told him about the final room.

"It's worse than I imagined, then," he sighed.

"I'm afraid so, Gibbs," Harden broke in. "We arrived just in time. I'm afraid this mission is over all of our heads, my friends, and it's undoubtedly about to get worse. We need to get back to the Academy immediately and alert the Alpha Team before—" Harden was cut off by a crack that split the very air like thunder. Paddy and Fankin both froze, as if they'd felt the crack in their very souls.

"What was tha'?" Kryda's question was directed more to the cosmos than her companions. Fankin was the first to recover and tentatively offered an answer.

CHAPTER 15

"It...felt like a break in a spell," he breathed, trembling. "But it must have been powerful, because I can usually only feel my own. And it *hurt*."

"It did indeed. That was more than merely a ward; it was a *seal*, and whatever was behind it is about to break free." Paddy's voice was flat.

"Looks like there dunae be any time fer reinforcements after all, Harden," Kryda said dryly, adjusting her pickaxe and lifting her chin in defiance, prepared for whatever challenge lay ahead. Harden looked to each member in turn, and saw the same determination in each of them.

Kurt stepped forward. "We have to do this, Harden, ready or not. The lives of everyone in the city may depend on it."

Harden let out a long breath, then turned to Gibbs. "You need to go for help, Gibbs. Hand me that saddlebag, then take my horse and go as fast as she'll carry you. Tell the gate guards that we need the Alpha Team immediately, and give them our location." He pulled his rapier from the saddlebag, affixing it confidently to his side. "We'll hold this off the best we can until they get here."

Gibbs hesitated, clearly wanting to follow the adventurers back into the sewers, but then nodded his acknowledgement and prepared to mount Harden's steed. Before he did so, he paused again. "Oh! I nearly forgot!"

Gibbs slung his tattered knapsack off his shoulder, digging hastily through the documents packed inside, before tugging something bulky and *heavy* from its depths and presenting it triumphantly to Kryda. "I picked it up from the blacksmith for you," he told her, barely managing to keep his footing as she nearly bowled him over with a bear hug, before accepting the freshly-forged Urgrosh with palpable glee.

"Thank'e, Gibbs!" she cried.

"Yes, thank you," Harden added, dryly, "but please do hurry. We're on a tight schedule."

Chapter 16

The Final Battle

On their way back into the final room, the crew paused as Harden gave orders, outlining a basic plan.

"We don't have time for specifics, and we know very little of what we face in there. Fankin and Paddy—do you two each have an assistive spell readied?" They nodded in the affirmative. "Good. If things get bad in there, I'll give a signal. Paddy, you protect Odo, and Fankin, you'll be on me. Leeta, Kurt, and Kryda—you three are the sturdiest and most well-armoured, so I'm counting on you to protect each other. Understood?" He glanced at each of them, but looked more pointedly at the stubborn dwarf.

"Sounds like a piece o' honey cake, does it no'?" Kryda murmured to Leeta, who chuckled nervously and rolled her eyes.

However, no amount of mental preparation, or smelling salts, could have saved them from the stench that that was now permeating the whole sewer. Leeta, holding her breath for as long as she could, swung her sword frantically as she advanced, attempting to clear the entryway of the rapidly forming skeletons. She wasn't hitting them, but the threat presented by her flailing blade was enough to force them back and make room for the rest of the adventurers to enter and ready themselves for the fight to begin in earnest.

The moment the magic users had clear sightlines on their targets, the battle truly erupted. Fankin launched a missile of fire over Kryda's head, staggering the nearest skeleton. Kryda ducked as it roared overhead, even though she was in no real danger, considering the height difference.

Odo had already snuck into the fray through the shadowed edges of the room and nimbly dodged an arrow, disappearing behind a pillar. Paddy cursed as the halfling, who was supposed to be under his protection, vanished from his sight. Quickly surveying the rest of the fight, Paddy spotted a skeleton preparing to throw a dagger at Leeta, and quickly cast a simple spell to befuddle the offending foe. He was successful in diverting its attack; the dagger fell short of Leeta.

With Leeta and Kryda advancing, Kurt found an opening between them and rushed in, his greatsword catching two skeletons completely off guard. One of them crumbled to dust immediately, and the other one, badly hurt, dropped its weapon and turned to flee. Kurt quickly dodged back out of the way, leaving the damaged skeleton open to an enchanted stone from Leeta's sling. The stone exploded in its chest cavity, and the skeleton crumbled away to nothing.

Harden watched his pupils carefully from the rear of the pack. He was proud of how far they'd come, but he still worried that this battle would be beyond them. *Please let the reinforcements come quickly,* he thought to himself. He wanted desperately to be helping them in the front, but as always, his job was to keep them alive by seeing what they couldn't.

"Leeta! Toward me!" he shouted. She spun at the sound of his voice, but still took a glancing blow to her arm, though it was much less severe than it would have been without his warning. When her assailant was dealt with, she nodded gratefully in his direction before charging back into battle.

Paddy had fallen back to Harden for a better view of the battle, still attempting to locate their slippery rogue.

CHAPTER 16

"There," Harden said to him abruptly, pointing to a low platform at the far end of the vast room where the enemies were clustered. "Can you *reach* that far?" he asked, emphasizing the word to make it abundantly clear to the elf that he did not mean merely physical reach. Paddy steepled two fingers in front of his forehead and extended one hand toward the target. Eyes closed in concentration, he nodded silently.

"Do it," Harden commanded. "HOLD CLOSE!" he shouted to the rest of the party as Paddy began muttering to himself, quietly preparing the spell.

Hearing Harden's shout, the signal for a combined area-of-effect spell, Fankin looked back at the Captain for direction, then scrambled up a ledge to give himself a better vantage point. He flipped to the most recent entry in his spellbook, grateful not to have to waste any more time with trivial *pleasantries* in this horrid place. As he began chanting the spell, a thick fog began to roll over the far end of the room where Harden had aimed the attention of the two magic users. The rest of his crew seemed to be battling in slow motion as Harden studied the work of his two spellcasters.

The cluster of undead foes began to look around in confusion and alarm as the fog slowly surrounded them. One stumbled as if it had been hit, reeling around with an attack only to find an ally impaled upon the end of its blade. Similar mysterious offences continued to plague the skeletons, faster and faster, until the whole knot of them were in a frenzy as they flailed at each other. Harden smiled proudly at Fankin, impressed by the wizard's unusual growth in power during his short time training at the Academy, and laid an approving hand upon Paddy's shoulder as well.

But they did not have long to celebrate.

Amidst the khaos, a massive blob of a creature stood from its throne. Towering at least two hands over the heads of the skeletons, it bellowed in rage at its minions—with little effect. It huffed in frustration, mucus spraying from its nostrils, before lumbering over to a large golden disc suspended from a frame nearby. It hefted its huge club high over its head and brought it down upon the gong.

Fueled by its anger at the intruders, as well as the failure of its own minions, the force of the blow resulted in a sound wave that caused the skeletons to cower and cover what once had been their ears—a reflex that had been rendered completely unnecessary at least a few hundred years ago, by the looks of them, but one that they seemed to have retained nonetheless.

The room shuddered, debris falling on friend and foe alike. One skeleton was pulverized so thoroughly by a falling chunk of rock that he himself splintered into additional hazardous projectiles, and Harden ducked a shattered humorous that was headed straight for his heart. As the room continued to crumble, Odo's expert hiding skills were now a hindrance rather than a help, as the pillar he was perched upon began to topple. He leaped down to the floor near Paddy, but it was obvious that he would not make it clear of the pillar before it crashed down on his tiny little head.

Paddy, his magic almost completely depleted by this point, resorted to more physical means of saving his charge. He threw himself bodily at the halfling, tackling him away from the deadly beam, but suffering the blow himself as a result. Odo, dazed by the force of the tackle and stunned by his crewmate's resulting injury, nodded a quick thanks to his unconscious friend and hoped that he could be recovered, before taking advantage of the khaos to slip away to a new ambush-worthy hiding place.

Kryda was also impacted by the secondary rubble created by the pillar's collapse, only just after recovering her balance following the first downpour of debris, and a large chunk of rubble slammed into her thigh. She cursed in pain and hastily assessed the damage—she knew the injury would slow her down for a while, but nothing was broken. Harden called to her and pointed to the fallen pillar. It took a moment for her eyes to focus well enough through the dust to see the limp form of Paddy that was pinned underneath it.

With debris, arrows and spells flying by over her head, Kryda crawled to the pillar to check on her friend. He was in bad shape, but he was still alive, thank the gods. She began hacking away at the pillar with her pickaxe, hurling huge chunks to the side. Her years in the mines made her the perfect candidate for this rescue mission, with strength and skill enough to surgically extricate her mark. Once she had cleared away enough weight, she used her pickaxe as a wedge, jacking up the pillar just high enough to tug Paddy's

CHAPTER 16

unconscious form free of the bulk.

Reaching into her pouch, she removed the gem Ada had given her. She had been skeptical when the woman told her it had incredible healing powers, but she decided this was certainly a moment worth testing it. She wasn't entirely sure how it worked; the healer had never explained how to use it. Trusting her instincts, Kryda set the gem gently on Paddy's chest as it rose and fell in shallow, wheezing breaths. As she did so, the little blue shard began to glow with a watery light, reminiscent of sunlight playing on a gently lapping lake.

To her surprise, after only a few seconds, Paddy sucked in a breath, coughing and spluttering, then rolled onto his side, spitting out a mouthful of blood and red-stained pearly teeth. His grey cheeks were still sunken and flushed, though, and by the looks of him, he was still mostly out of it. When his coughing fit subsided, Kryda rolled him onto his back once again, pressing the gem more firmly into the small hollow at the middle of his ribcage. His breaths slowly began to come more easily, but she continued to hold him still, waiting for a more decisive sign of recovery. It seemed an eternity before he finally opened his eyes and struggled into a sitting position. Looking himself over in amazement, he glanced up at Kryda, puzzled. He looked himself over in amazement, then glanced up at Kryda, puzzled. She held up the still faintly glowing gem and shrugged wordlessly.

"She did say it'd work like magic," Paddy remarked, continuing to test his newly-rejuvenated body by stretching and flexing.

"That she did. I didnae believe her a' first," Kryda admitted. Her work done, she tried to stand and return to the fight, but collapsed back onto one knee, bracing her injured leg with a grimace.

"Looks like you could use some of that magic for yourself," Paddy laughed.

"Aye, I could at tha'." Kryda gingerly balanced the gem on her thigh and waited for it to do its work. Only a few seconds passed before she felt that enough of her strength had returned that she could stand back up to her full four feet of height, looking triumphant and battle-ready once more. Seizing the handle of her pickaxe, she gave the head of it a kick to dislodge it from the pillar and slung it over her shoulder. She reached out a hand to help

Paddy up, pulling him roughly back to his feet with probably a little more force than was necessary.

The battle itself had pressed away from them. Their comrades now had the enemy backed into a corner, having pressed them into a tight knot around the ogre and his gong. Fankin was pressing in on them with a magical barrier to compliment the physical line of his comrades. They couldn't hold out much longer, though, even with Harden now fully immersed in the fray whilst still shouting commands, even though he was essentially blind to all but the nearest enemies.

Kryda ran to take Harden's place in the skirmish, and Paddy took over reinforcement of the magical barrier from where he stood, just as Fankin's magic was nearly spent and he was beginning to think he was about to fail them all. He glanced over in relief at Paddy when he felt the power shift, and managed to flash his comrade a weak smile before slumping to his knees.

The brief blip in power allowed a single skeleton to escape the magical enclosure. It headed for the weakest link; Fankin, drained as he was, could only cower away, fearing the worst. He closed his eyes, accepting his fate and deeply regretting that he hadn't been strong enough to hold the enemy off on his own. When he heard the approaching clatter of bones, he expected the end, but it did not come. He opened his eyes and saw his bony assailant struggling with a cluster of thorny vines that had sprung up from the rocky ground below.

Paddy had noticed the escaped foe and summoned nature in a place long devoid of it to save his friend. The tendrils rapidly grew from troublesome weeds into choking brambles that soon began ripping the skeleton's reanimated bones apart from the inside. Its skull popped off its head and rolled across the floor, coming to a stop and standing perfectly upright directly in front of Fankin, a rare and familiar blue flower growing through the top. Paddy flashed a proud, knowing grin at Fankin before whirling back to the fight and knocking another skull off with the end of his staff.

Fankin was momentarily jealous of the elf's natural ability to transition between physical and magical attacks so seamlessly. He reached down and

CHAPTER 16

plucked the blue flower from the skull, rubbing it between his hands and inhaling the regenerative scent he hadn't experienced since leaving home. The fragrant odor was reminiscent, and his mind was briefly transported back to the small shack where his grandmother had given him one of these flowers, along with his first spark of magic. He felt his power returning, as if he were standing in a whole field of the magical blooms.

Meanwhile, Harden stood gratefully back as he passed off his position to Kryda.

"Lead here. I'll get a better view."

"Aye, Cap'n," she replied, then looked to Paddy and Fankin. "Press on! Split the mob. We're goin' to get the big bloke! Le's finish this!"

With both magicians back in play, they were able to split the barrier in two as the fighters forced a divide through the center of their foes. It was slow going, but it gave Harden time to more clearly assess their situation. He was shocked to see Fankin and Paddy both refreshed, as if they'd been drawing from a crystal this whole time. As expected, the only crew member he couldn't immediately spot was Odo. He didn't know exactly *where* to look, but he did know *how* to look for the stealthy halfling, and it didn't take him too long to find the trail of notches the lithe rogue had left for that very reason.

When Harden finally caught a glimpse of the rogue, he couldn't comprehend how Odo had gotten to where he'd ended up. Shaking his head with a chuckle, he surveyed the area, mulling over Odo's vantage point and potential targets. He was both pleased and impressed that Odo had managed to put himself in a perfect position for a deadly aerial strike on the ogre, if the others could distract the beast from its rage-fuelled flailing for long enough to provide the rogue with a suitable opening. Harden and Odo made eye contact just long enough to wordlessly communicate that thought.

Kryda, Leeta, and Kurt had nearly made it to the ogre, but they held back just enough to create a bottleneck, allowing only a few skeletons at a time to advance through the connected barriers, which permitted the crew to pick them off one by one. Fankin was standing back, hurling spells into the trapped masses at either side and dwindling their numbers there as well. There were still too many, however, and the magic users were quickly becoming drained once again.

"Leeta, Kryda, Kurt, finish the split and get to the ogre. Fankin, we need him to stop moving once he's facing me. Paddy; hold on to that barrier. We're almost there!" Harden shouted. His team went to work, the bulbous crescent barrier closing off entirely into two separate domes, leaving only a few straggling skeletons for Kurt and the women to finish off. The hail of magical projectiles inside the domes ceased as Fankin prepared a growth to entangle the huge beast. The ogre paid absolutely no notice to the brambles growing around its massive feet, but as the melee fighters took out the last of the skeletal guards, it began to stamp a thunderous dance of rage as it advanced on Kurt, Leeta, and Kryda. They spotted Odo just as he readied his attack, grinning as he held a finger to his lips and then gestured to the ogre.

"Oi, jobby!" Kryda hollered at the beast, hoping to distract it until Odo could strike, "What the bloody 'ell is that oan yer neck?!" Feigning a comical combination of shock, concern, and disgust, she placed her free hand on her chest, pressing her tongue between her teeth and making a face at the lumbering ogre. "Aw, right then, it's jist yer heid, ain't it no'?"

It was doubtful if the beast actually understood her; even her mates only caught the gist of what she was saying beneath her comically broad accent, but her mocking did the trick anyhow. The monster roared in her face and reached out both its arms to grab at her, but she simply smiled gleefully at it as Fankin's barbed brambles sprung up from the ground, halting the ogre's attack and bringing it to its knees. When Kryda took a breath for her next line, she choked for a moment at the stench of the beast, which practically radiated off its monstrous form and added to the already horrid smell of the room.

"Howlin! Odo, I think it do be time to rid this poor critter of this vile, offencive bulge atop 'is neck!" she cried. Odo clearly agreed. Leaping from his perch upon the wall, he soared down toward the beast's head. Just as he did so, Leeta knocked off its helm with the butt of her blade, then whirled her sword around to slice up across its monstrous chest. At the very same moment, Odo's strike hit true, the halfling's dagger piercing through the top

CHAPTER 16

of its skull.

Unfortunately, they had all underestimated just how thick this particular skull was, and Odo's tiny blade wasn't enough to finish the job on its own. Kryda swung her pickaxe, but the old thing had been damaged under the pillar. The handle snapped as the tool struck, leaving its impact severely lacking. The beast was still struggling, and Fankin's bramble trap had begun to snap as the ogre strained against its restraints. The dome barriers were weakening as well as Paddy continued to empty his limited magic into maintaining them, there was very little time left for the adventurers to finish the battle.

Kryda drew her Urgrosh for the first time, not yet having had time to practice with it since Gibbs had picked it up for her, but confident in its use nonetheless. Enjoying the weight of it, she brought it 'round just in time to defend herself as the ogre freed one arm from the vines and reached out to grab her. The attack was a truly poor decision on the ogre's part—as it reached for Kryda, Kurt brought down his greatsword and severed its arm cleanly at the elbow joint.

Kryda's Urgrosh never ceased momentum as she spun it deftly around to its spear end, while Leeta twirled her wrist expertly to bring her blade into a piercing position. Before the ogre could get to its feet, both women drove their weapons straight through its chest, taking advantage of the chink in its breastplate where Leeta had slashed through it earlier. The force of their dual blow pushed the ogre's body backward, with a sickening crunch emanating from its legs as they were twisted and broken by the dead weight now bearing down upon them.

Odo watched as the ogre's severed arm twitched beside him and noticed a glowing bracer clasped around its wrist. When Leeta and Kryda struck, the arm's frenetic movements suddenly stopped, and the bracelet's glow began to falter. Odo reached down and removed the magical item from the ogre's log-sized arm; as he did so, the glow winked out entirely and the few remaining skeletons left in the domes collapsed. Paddy and Fankin gratefully released the barriers, and they too collapsed. For a moment, the room was completely silent as the adventurers paused to catch their breath.

After their momentary breather, they all gathered around the corpse of the ogre, in shock and pride at what they'd accomplished.

"Awa' n bile yer heid," Kryda hissed, breaking the silence. She spat on the corpse and wiped her brow of blood as she and Leeta retrieved their weapons from the dead ogre's massive torso. Leeta casually wiped the blood from her sword and resheathed it, while Kryda stared down at her Urgrosh, completely enamored by what she'd accomplished with the brand-new weapon.

"Looks like that fancy gadget was just what you needed, Kryda!" Leeta laughed and slapped a hand down on her shoulder, breaking her lovestruck trance.

"Aye. It feels…familiar," she replied, smiling, and looked back at Harden, who was practically bursting with pride like a mother hen at his crew of adventurers.

"More like the weight of your pickaxe that you're used to," Harden replied, nodding briefly and returning her smile.

"Must be it," Kryda murmured halfheartedly, not at all convinced that her surprising proficiency with a brand-new weapon was quite that simple. She walked over to a tapestry on the wall and ripped it down, using it to wipe her weapon clean and sneezing at the dust that puffed off of the ancient cloth as she did so.

Odo was the first to notice that the stone behind the tapestry Kryda had torn down was cut differently from the others in the room. "Kryda, look there," he called, pointing out the area. "You know a fair bit about stone, don't you?"

"Where's ye lookin'?" she asked, approaching the wall curiously and running her calloused fingers over it, searching. "Ah, ye've got somethin' there…" She broke off as her fingers dipped into a rough depression in the wall. She probed further, and found that the anomaly was deceptively deep. "Aha!" she grinned, grasping the stone and pulling it backwards.

As she did so, the oddly coloured portion of the wall shifted with a dull grating, revealing a door. Kryda beckoned to the others, who quickly ran over to help her heave open the massive stone door. They peered into the opening, their eyes adjusting slowly to the murky darkness. The space was

CHAPTER 16

dazzling, filled with dark crystals that glinted with eerie light gleaming from a floating orb in the center of the hidden chamber.

Fankin spoke first. "I don't think any of us need a spell to tell us that this room is unnatural."

"And although the battle we just fought wasn't either," Harden began, stroking his chin, "this is certainly more intricate."

"Definitely not the work of a brainless ogre," Leeta added.

Kryda chuckled. "Fer one, the bugger couldn'ta fit through tha' door."

They all laughed, but stopped as they noticed Harden's face hardening into a grim line. He glanced at each of them in turn. "You all did well today, and we have certainly won a victory here, but don't be fooled. This isn't over."

Making their way back through the previously *sealed* room, they were greeted by another crew. The reinforcements that were sent all looked out of place in their gleaming armour and greenish pallor. Connahay stared at Harden for a moment, unable to hide the shock of what he was seeing before him, then gave the signal for his troops to clear out. One held back just long enough to nod at Kryda and the others with respect.

Chapter 17

The Disappearance

"The city will forever be in your debt, Harden." The Governor set down Harden's report and leaned back in his heavily-cushioned desk chair, glancing approvingly up at the Captain as he carefully straightened the stack of papers.

"It was all due to the hard work and bravery of my team, Governor. This mission proved to be one better suited for adventurers well above their rank, but they rose to face the challenge with admirable courage and persistence. The retired adventurer Gibbs deserves credit for his aid in this venture as well—we might not have made it out of those sewers if it weren't for his research, warnings and last minute delivery."

"Yes, we'll see that he is recognized as well." The Governor nodded officiously, then dropped the facade of professionalism and smiled at Harden. "Seems his crazy ramblings weren't all that crazy after all, eh? You really think today's incident is connected to his previous findings?"

"Without question, sir, and if I may, I think you may need to make a public statement on this matter. People will need to be prepared for what is undoubtedly coming."

"We don't want to cause a panic, Harden, but I will certainly see that our city guards, and of course our healers, are prepared with all of the information we currently possess. Speaking of which—how is the cleanup coming along, Ada?"

The elder healer of Starting City rose from the chair where she'd been sitting quietly, her keen blue eyes studying Harden intently as if she could sense more to his words than what he'd spoken. She answered the Governor promptly, but her eyes remained on the Captain. "The cleansing of the sewers is progressing well, but that is only the beginning; is it not, young man?" She leaned forward, her blue eyes still boring into his. Harden nodded, his face grim.

"I fear it may be both a beginning and an end."

* * *

"OHO! There 'e be, tha man o' the hour! Our fearless leader, 'n hero teh all o' Starting City!" Kryda hiccuped, pounding her mug heavily on the table and sloshing ale everywhere, before raising it high in the air as Harden approached the group.

"Ah, Kryda. Drunk already, I see," he huffed, chuckling. "Well, you deserve it—you all do. You lot are the real heroes here. You didn't back down, even knowing that reinforcements may never have come, and in doing so you showed more courage than many an adventurer of much higher rank."

The team all raised their glasses to that and clinked them together, grateful to each other for the teamwork that had carried them through their ordeal. Harden placed a hand on Kryda's head and ruffled her hair, then smirked crookedly and pushed her playfully back into her chair before seating himself beside her.

Harden wasn't particularly happy that his team had begun celebrating so

CHAPTER 17

soon after exhausting themselves so thoroughly, but he couldn't deny them a bit of fun after the tenacity they'd shown earlier that day. Paddy and Fankin were wearing large energy crystals strung around their necks, which ebbed and glowed with magical energy. Even after a good nap beside the Valanian crystal, their reserves were still depleted; but after word of their battle had spread, it had been fairly easy for them to obtain some new magical items from grateful shopkeepers—including their new necklaces.

Kryda had come straight back to the tavern after their battle, but Eilatra had previously assured Harden that she'd made the impetuous dwarf relax in a special bath and convince her to take a nap. Still, she must have started to make quick work of the tavern's supply of ale as soon as she'd awoken.

Leeta and Odo, being more reasonable than the dwarf, looked quite refreshed after returning to the barracks for a proper sleep, but still seemed a little worse for wear. Leeta's garb was meticulous as usual, but when Harden looked closely, he could see that her forehead was somewhat more creased and her eyes more troubled than they had been the day before. As for Odo, the halfling was always fairly laconic, but he seemed even less talkative than usual as he nursed his mug of ale.

Weary as they were, the crew's merrymaking didn't last as long as it usually did. They quickly began to retire one by one to catch some well-deserved sleep, looking forward to the lie-in and day off that they'd been promised following their adventure. Harden was also exhausted, but he remained in the tavern until everyone but Kryda had gone. The Captain was fairly relieved when Eilatra finally offered to see the dwarf back to her room.

"Ah'm fine," Kryda slurred in protest, fumbling and nearly dropping her stein.

"Kryda, you're going to waste that ale," Eilatra scolded her. "It's time for you to go upstairs and catch some sleep. I'll make sure your wineskin is filled and chilled for the morning, alright? Harden has had a long day, too, so let's give him his leave as well."

Kryda took a long hard look at Harden, realizing even in her inebriated state that Eilatra was right about him, at least. He looked like he'd aged ten years. In his eyes, she saw pride, but also a great deal of worry.

"Go on to bed, Kryda. You deserve a good rest," he told her gently, noting her scrutiny.

"Ay, as do ye. We woulnae made it tru if it weren't fer you leadin' us the way ye did," Kryda mumbled, raising her half-empty stein to the Captain.

Harden wanted to protest; he still felt guilty for leading his crew into a battle far beyond their capabilities, but he merely nodded, encouraging her to go with Eilatra. He watched them go until they turned the corner, then slumped back in his chair with a sigh and rested his head in his hands, ruffling his sandy hair, then stroking it neatly back into place. He straightened back up and drew in a deep breath before getting up to leave.

* * *

Eilatra knew she'd never get Kryda up the stairs in this state, so she led the dwarf to an empty room in the workers' quarters around the back of the tavern. She opened the window to air out the long-unused room, only half-listening to Kryda, who was drunkenly mumbling to her about nothing in particular. Leaving the door to Kryda's new room open so she could keep one ear trained on the dwarf, she collected the kitchen scraps to take out to the compost, quickly popping her head into the room to tell Kryda she'd be right back.

Kryda could hear Eilatra humming to herself through the window and began to drift off. Feeling a sudden chill, she stumbled to her feet and headed over to close the window. The breeze from outside wasn't cold, but there was something else in the air, something that made the hair on the back of her neck stand up. Taking a deep breath, she attempted to shake off the fog that shrouded her brain. Her senses were still muddled, but she listened closely—and heard nothing. No owls, no crickets, no nocturnal city noises, and most importantly, no Eilatra. Kryda's breath caught in her throat.

"Eilly?" she whispered into the dark. There was no answer, but Kryda spotted a shadow moving at the edge of the building. She rushed out of the

CHAPTER 17

room, seizing her Urgrosh from where Eilatra had propped it up by the door. She crept outside, searching for Eilatra's footprints. There were too many recent tracks for Kryda to pick out any particular set, so she instead headed in the direction she'd last heard the elf humming from, which led towards the stable. As she drew closer, she noticed that the previously sleeping horses had started to stir, their nostrils flaring. A soft but frantic voice was whispering to them in an attempt to calm them.

"Eilly!" Kryda whispered again, relieved to hear the elf's voice. Eilatra peeked her head out from the stable stall she had been crouched in.

"Kryda! Get back inside!" she hissed, her whisper barely audible, but she motioned emphatically to get her point across. Kryda shook her head and motioned for the elf to come to her instead, but Eilatra shook her head and waved her back again.

As she did so, a gutteral gurgling rose from the darkness of the trees behind the stable, low and sickeningly *wet*, like a lion's dull roar, but choked off and bubbling as if its throat had been slit. The noise reverberated in Kryda's uneasy stomach, and nausea rose hot and fast in her throat. The horses in the stable began to whinny in fear, stamping, their eyes rolling as they strained against their lines.

Kryda's eyes widened as a massive shadow emerged from the trees, branches snapping and trunks squealing as they were bent carelessly aside by the bulk of the towering shape. "Eilatra! Get out of there!" Kryda hissed, her tone sharp and urgent.

Eilatra looked conflicted for a moment. She glanced briefly at Kryda, deep fear in her gaze, but then turned away and began to release the horses. "Go!" she called to the terrified animals, giving the nearest freed horse a firm slap on its rump to spur it onward. Her encouragement, however, proved entirely unnecessary when the beast roared again. The other horses followed the first as quickly as Eilatra could release their clips.

Kryda rushed to the stable to retrieve her friend as fast as she could, unaware that Harden had heard the commotion as well and was now doing the same from the far edge of the building. Eilatra was at the back of the stable now, releasing the last horse. The shadowy beast had cleared the trees, its feet squelching into the earth with a thud as it stepped ever closer. Kryda had nearly reached Eilatra when the back of the stable was completely obliterated by a single sweep of the monster's hulking arm.

Eilatra screamed as she was flung headlong into a stall as if she weighed nothing more than a ragdoll. Kryda stumbled and fell as a chunk of what had previously been one of the stable's support beams knocked her feet right out from under her. When she looked up, a monstrous head was peering into the makeshift window it had created. Heart pounding, Kryda rolled out of sight into a mostly-intact stall and secured her grip on her Urgrosh.

She still felt weak and woozy, both from her drinking and her sudden fall, but she stumbled to her feet and leaped out of the stall, screaming at the beast to try and pull its attention away from Eilatra. The beast, however, was completely unperturbed—it hardly took notice of such an insignificant creature, and especially not when it already had its eye on a snack.

The enormous head pulled back from the gap just far enough to allow its giant hand to reach through. Its massive fingers closed around Eilatra, lifting her into the air as if she weighed nothing more than a sheet of parchment. She struggled to free herself from its grip, but to no avail. Watching her friend's predicament helplessly, Kryda shouted again and desperately flung her Urgrosh at the creature's arm. It howled in pain and dropped the girl, pulling its arm back from the massive hole in the side of the stable.

Kryda ran to Eilatra's side and helped her up just as Harden caught up to them. He nodded briefly to Kryda, then lifted the elven girl into his arms and prepared to carry her inside. As it turned out, Gibbs had also heard the commotion, and had come to check on Eilatra. He reached the back door of the stable just in time to watch as the monster's other arm came down and snatched Kryda into the air.

"Go!" Kryda screamed, kicking and flailing against the monster's grip as she was lifted completely out of the stable. "Get Eilatra out of here!" Harden hesitated. "Please! GO!" she cried. Harden glanced back at Kryda once more before turning and sprinting to Gibbs, carefully passing the injured barmaid into the elderly adventurer's arms. Gibbs secured his hold on her, but once he'd done so, he reached into his belt and pulled out a weathered old wand,

CHAPTER 17

firing a bolt of lightning at the beast and striking it in the shoulder.

It staggered back, wisps of smoke curling from its injured shoulder as it tried to recover its balance. As it flailed in pain, Kryda was lifted higher above her attacker's head then released unceremoniously. She managed to embed her pickaxe into the base of its neck before it spun around and slammed her far into the forest until she collided full-force with a tree trunk, shattering something in her torso. She managed to reach out one arm back towards her friends in desperation before the darkness consumed her, and she slumped down to the base of the tree.

"KRYDA!!" Eilatra screamed, hot, angry tears spilling from her eyes. She struggled against Gibbs' hold, desperately trying to go to Kryda, but Harden quickly seized her other arm, and the two men held her back.

Having dealt with one of the little nuisances at its feet, the beast now turned its attention to them, and began advancing. Fortunately, the commotion had attracted a sizeable group of adventurers, who began gathering behind Harden. The Captain was only vaguely aware of his own crew forming up behind him, awaiting his orders. Harden's attention was elsewhere; he was trying to think of a way to reach Kryda.

Eilatra wrenched herself free from the two men, but was quickly restrained by several others, who led the sobbing elf back into the tavern. Gibbs laid a hand on Harden's shoulder, his gaze steely with determination as his eyes met the Captain's. Inspired by the old man's fearlessness, Harden summoned his own. He looked back at the beast and shouted the fiercest battle cry he'd ever uttered. The rousing call was quickly answered by the shouts of the warriors behind him, and the group surged forward toward the monster.

Inside the tavern, an old woman was wrapping Eilatra's wounded leg with trembling hands. The elf's ears trembled as she listened intently to the chaos that had erupted, and she bowed her head, her lips moving in the barest whisper.

"I'll find you."

END

About the Author

Megan MacLean is a budding author steeped in pen and paper role play and fantasy worlds. She began writing novels at a very young age, never able to keep it brief with entire worlds blooming in her mind the moment she was prompted to tell a fictional story. Kryda's Adventures series is one such world, stemming from multiple role playing scenarios that brought the main character and the world around her to life. She has participated in the yearly NANOWRIMO (National Novel Writing Month) since 2009 which kept the ideas and passion flowing while also balancing the many demands of family life.

Made in the USA
Monee, IL
25 February 2021